William Powell Frith

John Leech His Life and Work
Volume 2

William Powell Frith

John Leech His Life and Work
Volume 2

1st Edition | ISBN: 978-3-75238-846-6

Place of Publication: Frankfurt am Main, Germany

Year of Publication: 2020

Outlook Verlag GmbH, Germany.

Reproduction of the original.

JOHN LEECH

His Life and Work

BY

WILLIAM POWELL FRITH

VOL. II.

CHAPTER I.

"PUNCH."

In the year 1841 I exhibited a picture at the Suffolk Street Gallery, and I recollect accidentally overhearing fragments of a conversation between a certain Joe Allen and a brother member of the Society of British Artists in Suffolk Street. Allen's picture happened to hang near mine, and we were both "touching up" our productions. Joe Allen was the funny man of the society, and, though he startled me a little, he did not surprise me by a loud and really good imitation of the peculiar squeak of Punch.

"Look out, my boy," he said to his friend, "for the first number. We" (I suppose he was a member of the first staff) "shall take the town by storm. There is no mistake about it. We have so-and-so"—naming some well-known men—"for writers; Hine, Kenny Meadows, young Leech, and a lot more first-rate illustrators," etc.

Whether Allen's friend took his advice and bought the first number of *Punch*, which appeared in the following July, I know not; but I bought a copy, and remember my disappointment at finding Leech conspicuous by his absence from the pages. In the hope of finding him in the second issue, I went to the shop where I had bought the first. The shopman met my request for the second number of *Punch*, as well as I can recollect, in the following words:

"What paper, sir? Oh, *Punch*! Yes, I took a few of the first; but it's no go. You see, they billed it about a good deal" (how well I recollect that expression!), "so I wanted to see what it was like. It won't do; it's no go."

I have been told that, like most newspapers, *Punch* had some difficulty in keeping upon his legs in his first efforts to move; but as those elegant members, so exquisitely drawn by Tenniel, have supported the famous hunchback for nearly half a century, there is no need for his friends' anxiety as to his future movements.

Though Leech had engaged himself to the then proprietors of *Punch* as one of the illustrators of the paper, it seems strange that his first contribution did not appear till the 7th of August, and in the fourth number, and stranger still that its appearance should have damaged the paper. Under the heading of "Foreign Affairs," the artist represents groups of foreigners such as may be seen any day in the neighbourhood of Leicester Square. The reader is told in a footnote that the plate does not represent foreign *gentlemen*, an unnecessary intimation to anyone who knows a foreign gentleman.

2

It is said that this engraving sent down the circulation of *Punch* to an alarming point. I confess my inability to understand this, and would rather attribute the decadence to some other cause, contemporary with the production of "Foreign Affairs." The drawing is somewhat hard upon the foreign frequenters of the purlieus of Leicester Square, and would only have been more acceptable to John Bull on that account. By Leech's non-appearance in *Punch* for many months after "Foreign Affairs" was published, one is driven to the conclusion that the managers had little faith in him as an attraction. The second volume contains very few of Leech's designs, while it bristles with inferior work.

My own admiration for Leech's genius, so constantly roused by his works, with which I was familiar, created a great desire for his acquaintance; but being perfectly unknown at that time as an artist, and knowing none of Leech's friends, I began to despair of the realization of my wishes, when accident helped me.

A Scottish painter—a Highlander and fierce Jacobite—named McIan, who was also an actor and friend of Macready, to whose theatrical company he was attached, lived with his wife, an accomplished artist, somewhere in the neighbourhood of Gordon Square. Calling one morning to see Mrs. McIan, I found her in her studio, not, as usual, hard at work at her own easel, but superintending the labours of a pupil, who was hard at work at another; and the pupil, a tall, slim, and remarkably handsome young man, was John Leech.

I made some remark about the different method in which he was employed to that with which he was familiar. I forget what he was copying—some still life, I think.

"I like painting much better than what I have to grind at day after day, if I could only do it," said Leech; "but it's so confoundedly difficult, you know, and requires such a lot of patience."

I fancy I thought his efforts in oil-painting on that occasion very promising; but the exigencies of his position quite prevented the unceasing devotion to the study of painting which is required before any success can be assured.

Leech was once heard to say that he would rather be the painter of a really good picture than the producer of any number of the "kind of things" he did. I, for one, am very thankful that he never did produce a good picture, for he would have been tempted to repeat the success, to the loss of numbers of delightful sketches.

Mrs. McIan appeared to think that Leech would soon cease to draw for *Punch*; indeed, she doubted, as did many others, that *Punch* would long succeed in attracting the public; and I joined her in the hope—rather hypocritically, I fear—that her young friend would persevere in mastering the

3

difficulty of the technicalities of oil-painting, and thus place himself amongst the best painters of the country. Leech had taken many lessons from Mrs. McIan, and that lady seemed convinced that he had but to persevere and the difficulties would fall before him, as, to use her own figure, the walls of Jericho fell before the sound of the trumpet. Ah, perseverance! "there's the rub."

From the time of my introduction to Leech I became gradually very intimate with him, and the more I knew of his nature, the more I became convinced that he totally lacked the disposition for continuous, steady, mechanical industry necessary for success in painting. He constantly ridiculed the care spent on the details in pictures; finish, in his opinion, was so much waste of time. "When you can see what a man intends to convey in his picture, you have got all he wants, and all you ought to wish for; all elaboration of an idea after the idea is comprehensible is so much waste of time"—this was his constant cry, a little contradicted by the fact that he as constantly tried to paint his ideas, but in a fitful and perfunctory manner.

I can imagine the enthusiasm that was lighted up in Leech upon his first sight of one of our annual exhibitions. After a visit to one of them he was known to have gone home, and getting out easel, canvas, and colours, he would set to work in a fury of enthusiasm, which evaporated at the encounter of the first technical difficulty. He used to take pleasure in watching my own attempts at painting, and I remember on one occasion, when I was finishing a rather elaborate piece of work, he said:

"Ah, my Frith, I wasn't created to do that sort of thing! I should never have patience for it."

He was right, and, happily for the world, he became convinced that, even if he had the power to fully "carry out"—as we call it—one of his drawings into a completed oil picture, the time required would have deprived us of immortal sketches; and though he undoubtedly "left off where difficulties begin"—as I once heard a painter, who was exasperated at Leech's sneers at his manipulation, say to him—he has left behind him work which will continue to delight succeeding generations so long as wit, humour, character and beauty are appreciated—that is to say, so long as human nature endures.

I feel I ought to apologize for what I am about to tell, because it has nothing to do with my hero beyond the fact of its occurrence having taken place on the memorable morning when I first had the happiness of meeting him.

I have said that McIan was a Scotchman, a Highlander of the clan McIan, and a worshipper of Charles Stuart, whose usual cognomen, the Pretender, I should have been sorry to have used in the presence of my Jacobite friend. As

4

Leech left the room to go to his "grind," as he called his woodwork, McIan entered, and we were discussing Leech's prospects when McIan's servant—an old, hard-featured Scotchwoman—hurried into the room, and, in an awe-stricken voice, said:

"Sir—sir, here's the Preences!"

The words were scarcely out of her mouth, when two gentlemen entered—tall, rather distinguished but melancholy, looking young men. No sooner did McIan and his wife catch sight of them, than, without a word, they both dropped upon their knees, and while the lady kissed the hands of one of the gentlemen, her husband paid a similar attention to the hands of the other. I was holding my hat, and I remember I dropped it in my astonishment, for I was not aware that I was in the presence of the last of the Stuarts; or that these two young men claimed to be the great-grandsons of the hero of Culloden, and amongst a large section of Scotchmen, and not a few Englishmen, had their claim allowed. Anyone curious about this delusion can read for himself how it was dispelled, but the men themselves implicitly believed in their royal descent. They are both dead now. I once saw one of them again at a garden-party at Chelsea Hospital, where his likeness to the Stuarts was the talk of the company. It was certainly striking.

It is a melancholy task to me to try to recall the social scenes in which Leech so often figured—sad indeed to think how few of his friends, more intimate with him than I, now remain amongst us! Though Leech very seldom illustrated any ideas but his own, I can recall an example or two to the contrary; and still oftener have I seen, by the sparkle of his eye, that something occurring in conversation had suggested a "cut."

I think it was Dickens who said that a big cock-pheasant rising in covert under one's nose was like a firework let off in that locality. Elsewhere we have Leech's rendering of the idea.

When cards, or some other way of getting rid of time after dinner, had been proposed, I have heard Leech say:

"Oh, bother cards! Let us have conversation."

And talk it was, often good talk; but Leech was more a listener than a partaker. Not that he could not talk, and admirably; but he was always on the watch for subjects which he hoped something in conversation might suggest.

Leech's mental condition was certainly deeply tinged with the sadness so common to men who possess wit and humour to a high degree. He sang well, but his songs were all of a melancholy character, and very difficult to get from him. Indeed, the only one I can remember, and that but partially, was something about "King Death," with allusions to a beverage called "coal-black wine," which that potentate was supposed to drink. As I write I can see the dear fellow's melancholy face, with his eyes cast up to the ceiling, where Dickens said the song was written in ghostly characters which none but Leech could read.

I may give another example—rare, no doubt—of Leech's having used a suggested subject. Many years ago my brother-in-law, long since dead, took a party of friends to the Derby. They drove, or, rather, were driven, down to Epsom, the usual post-boy being recommended as a careful, steady driver—a character very desirable, considering the crowded state of the road, more especially on the return journey. The post-boy quite realized all that was said of him as the party went to the course, but when the time came for departure he was found, after considerable searching, to be as nearly dead-drunk as possible. What was to be done? The man could scarcely stand; his driving was, of course, out of the question.

THE DRUNKEN POST-BOY.

"Well," said my brother-in-law to his friends, "if you will trust yourselves to me, I will ride and drive you back;" and, after tying the post-boy on to the carriage, where he soon fell fast asleep, my brother mounted and drove his party safely home.

This I thought a good subject for Leech, and I suggested it to him. He smiled faintly, and said not a word. Very nearly a year after I had told him of the incident, as I was walking with him one day, he said:

"By the way, Frith, are you going to use the subject you mentioned to me of the drunken post-boy and your brother-in-law?"

"I? No," said I; "it's more in your way than mine."

"Then I'll do it next week."

He was as good as his word.

Nothing could be less like my brother-in-law than the delightful "swell" who is driving home some charming women, who are, however, left to our imagination; and as to the post-boy, the artist has awoke him to some purpose. What could surpass that drunken smile?

THEY MAY BE OFFICERS BUT THEY ARE NOT GENTLEMEN.

Long, long ago there might have been seen on the sands at Ramsgate two stuffed figures, the size of life, intended to represent soldiers; for they were bedecked with the red coat, cap, and trousers of the ordinary private. The clothes were simply stuffed out into something resembling human forms, but the effect, as may be supposed, was ludicrous in the extreme. They were the work of a professor of archery, who supplied his customers with bows and arrows, with which the archer showed how seldom he could hit the target made by the two soldiers. Leech and I watched the shooting for some time, till the little sketch-book was produced, and Leech made a rapid drawing of the two soldiers, afterwards to figure in an inimitable cut in *Punch*.

A young lady is seen bathing with her aunt, whose attention she is directing to the two stuffed figures. The aunt is short-sighted, and the girl is wickedly pretending that the figures are live officers, watching the bathers. The aunt says, "They may be officers, but they are not gentlemen," etc.

I am sure that Leech never used a model, in the sense that the model is commonly used by artists, for the thousands of human beings made immortal by his genius; but that he made numberless sketches for backgrounds, detail of dresses, landscapes, foregrounds, and bits of character caught from unconscious sitters, there can be no doubt. How wonderful was the memory, how sensitive the mental organization, that could retain and reproduce every variety of type, every variety of beauty and character!

CHAPTER II.

CARTOONS.

As I fancy I am one of the few of Leech's friends who have figured personally in *Punch*, I may be excused for the egotism of the following:

About the year 1852 I began the first of a series of pictures from modern life, then quite a novelty in the hands of anyone who could paint tolerably. When the picture which was called "Many Happy Returns of the Day" (a birthday subject, in which the health of the little heroine of the day is being drunk) was finished, Leech came to see it, and expressed his satisfaction on finding an artist who could leave what he called "mouldy costumes" for the habits and manners of everyday life. As he was speaking, two of my brother artists, whose practice was on different lines to mine, called, and saw my picture for the first time. They both looked attentively at it, and the longer they looked—judging from their faces—the less they liked it. I shall not forget Leech's expression when I gave him a sort of questioning look as to the correctness of his judgment.

"Well, what do you think of the picture?" said Leech to one of the painters.

"Well, really I don't know what to think," was the reply.

It never occurred to me that the incident was one likely to serve my friend for a drawing; lively was my surprise, and great was my pleasure, therefore, when I saw myself "immortalized for ever," as my old master used to say, in the pages of *Punch*.

In this drawing may be seen a striking proof of the avoidance of personality which always distinguished Leech. I cannot see my own back, but I have been assured by those who have had that privilege that there is a dashing, not to say aristocratic, character about Jack Armstrong to which I have no claim. While Messrs. Potter and Feeble are quite curiously unlike the persons they are supposed to represent—neither of my high art friends wore beards—yet the attitudes of the men were exactly reproduced; while the background, with armour, oak-cabinet, etc., for which no sketch was taken, was a perfectly correct representation of my old painting-room.

"JACK ARMSTRONG."

In one of my autumnal holidays Leech stayed a few days with me. He had not been well; picking up "a thousand stones in a thousand hours," to which he likened his unceasing work, had begun to tell upon him; and in reply to my warning, that, for his own sake, to say nothing of the interests of *Punch*, he should husband his strength—for, I added, "If anything happened to you, who are 'the backbone of *Punch*,' what would become of the paper?"—I can see his smile as I hear him say, "Don't talk such rubbish! backbone of *Punch*, indeed! Why, bless your heart! there isn't a fellow at work upon the paper that doesn't think *that* of himself, and with about as much right and reason as I should. *Punch* would get on well enough without me, or any of those who think themselves of such importance."

Among the many admirable qualities that adorned the character of John Leech his modesty was remarkable; he thought little or nothing of his own work. "Talk of drawing, my dear fellow," he once said to me, "what is my drawing compared to Tenniel's? Look at the way that chap can draw a boot; why, I couldn't do it to save my life."

Though Leech in his modesty chose to ignore the fact, it was no less a fact that for nearly a quarter of a century he was the leading spirit of *Punch*. "Think," said Thackeray, "what a number of *Punch* would be without a drawing by Leech in it!"

In addition to the wonderful political cartoons, Leech contributed more than three thousand illustrations of life and manners to the paper; and it is said—I know not how truly—that he received from first to last more than £40,000 for his contributions to *Punch* alone. If he did, what did he do with the money? That he was in no way extravagant I know, and that he was frequently in dire straits after his connection with *Punch* I also know. Let my reader imagine what pecuniary trouble must have been to this man, whose mind was racked by the constantly recurring demands for intellectual work such as Leech supplied week after week, and often day after day! Did he lend or give away his hardly-earned money? Did he accept bills for so-called friends, and find that he had to meet them? Leech was one of the most open-hearted and generous of men, an easy victim to a plausible tale of real or fictitious distress. I suppose we shall never know why a man who made so large an income, who had not a large family to absorb much of it, and who never lived expensively, should have died comparatively poor. Let me leave these painful considerations and "pursue the triumph and partake the gale" of the artist's glorious career.

Between Cruikshank and Leech there existed little sympathy and less intimacy. The extravagant caricature that pervades so much of Cruikshank's work, and from which Leech was entirely free, blinded him a little to the great merit of Cruikshank's serious work. I was very intimate with "Immortal George," as he was familiarly called, and I was much surprised by the coolness with which he received my enthusiastic praise of Leech.

"Yes, yes," said George, "very clever. The new school, you see. Public always taken with novelty."

For the larger part of fifty-seven years Cruikshank told me he had been in the habit of drinking wine and spirits, often a great deal too much of both; but from his fifty-seventh birthday to his seventy-fifth, when he lectured me for taking a single glass of sherry, he had devoted himself to strict teetotalism, the interests of which he advocated by tongue, brush, and etching-needle.

Unlike Leech, Cruikshank was a painter, and the last years of his life were spent in painting a huge picture, or, rather, a series of pictures upon one canvas, which he called "The Worship of Bacchus." From this work he executed a large engraving, a proof of which he presented to me, telling me to study it well and I should see what dire results might arise from drinking a glass of sherry. Like most proselytes, Cruikshank carried his faith in his creed to the verge of absurdity, and sometimes beyond it; but in the "Worship of Bacchus," and more powerfully still in a series of etchings called "The Bottle," he gave his tragic power full play, and produced scenes and incidents in which the consequences of "drink" are portrayed—now with pathos, now with the terrible retribution that often ends the drunkard's career in madness.

In one of the large cartoons in *Punch* Leech used the awful figure of "Fagin in the Condemned Cell" (one of Cruikshank's finest illustrations to "Oliver Twist"), changing him into King Louis Philippe. That sovereign was always somewhat of a red rag to Leech, as many cuts, in which the king is turned into ridicule, prove; and when the crash of 1848 came, Leech received the fugitive with a shower of drawings, culminating in the tragic figure exiled and in the condemned cell. The student of Leech does not require to be told that the artist was as great in the tragedies of life as he was when he shot the follies as they flew about him, or when he touched so caressingly the beauty of childhood and of women.

During the Crimean War, when such fearful news came to us of the sufferings of our soldiers during the inclement winter of 1854-55, the Emperor of Russia is said to have invoked the aid of Generals January and February in our ruin. Those officers certainly destroyed many of our men, but one of them laid his icy hand upon the man who had called him for so different a purpose. Never can I forget the impression that Leech's drawing of the Emperor's death-bed made upon me! There lay the Czar, a noble figure in death, as he was in life, and by his side a stronger King than he—a bony figure, in General's uniform, snow-besprinkled, who "beckons him away." Of all Leech's serious work, this seems to me the finest example. Think how savage Gillray or vulgar Rowlandson would have handled such a theme!—the Emperor would have been caricatured into a repulsive monster, and Death would have lost his terrors. Moreover, neither of those artists was capable of conceiving the subject.

To show the infinite variety of Leech's powers, I may draw attention in this place to another of the political cartoons.

The uneasiness created in this country by what was called the "Papal Aggression" always seemed to me as absurd and unfounded as it has since proved to have been. I remember asking Cardinal Manning, then Archbishop of Westminster by order of the Pope, for his autograph. He wrote his name for me, but when I asked him to add his title, he smiled and said, "I dare not do that; I might be sent to prison if I wrote my Popish title."

Lord John Russell was in power at that time, and was of course very active in the crusade against the Catholics. The Cardinal in England was Wiseman; and Leech drew Lord John as a street boy, running away from the Cardinal's door, after chalking "No Popery" upon it. Perfect in workmanship, and perfect in idea, is this admirable drawing.

I may note here one very bad consequence of the "Papal Aggression"— namely, the secession of Richard Doyle from the *Punch* staff. Doyle was a Catholic; it was therefore impossible for him to remain amongst men who, by pen and pencil, opposed what was called the audacious attempt to "tithe and toll in our dominions." It was a pity, for Doyle was, next to Leech, by far the strongest man on the staff of *Punch* artists—quaintly humorous, and full of a delicate fancy, but without the broad views of life or the grasp of character that distinguished Leech. Of course, as personality was the essence of the political cartoons, the use of it was unavoidable; but Leech managed to be personal without being offensive to the chief actor, unless, as in the case of Louis Philippe and a few others, he considered that their escapades deserved severe castigation; he then took good care to apply the whip with a will. Lord Russell, in his "Recollections," speaks of the "No Popery" satire as "a fair hit."

In many of the political cartoons official personages are represented as boys, well-behaved or ill-behaved, obstinate or stupid, or both, in the work appointed for them. For example, when Sir Robert Peel resigned, in 1846, Lord John Russell figures as page-boy applying for the vacant place. The Queen looks the button boy up and down, and then says, "I fear, John, you are not strong enough for the situation."

Then we have Disraeli, also as a boy, in whose figure that statesman's curious foppery in dress is felicitously noted, confronted with a majestic figure of Sir Robert Peel, who says:

"Well, my little man, what are you going to do this Session, eh?" "Why—aw—aw—I've made arrangements—aw—to smash everything."

Events of the past, looked at by the light of the present, assume sometimes very strange, almost incredible aspects. Can there have been a time, one is inclined to ask, when a man's religion could prove a bar to college, Bench, and Parliament? Assuredly there was such a time, and not long ago—say forty years or so—when no Jew could be a judge or a member of Parliament; and it was only after severe battles and many defeats that victory at last attended the Jewish banner. One of the most violent opponents of the Jews was Sir Robert Harry Inglis, a very conscientious and worthy gentleman. By a happy thought of Leech's, Sir Robert is made to figure in one of the most humorous of the political cartoons.

About this time my old friend Frank Stone had painted two pictures in illustration of his favourite theme—love. They were called "The First Appeal" and "The Last Appeal." In the first a kind of peasant lover is beseeching his "flame" to listen to his vows. She listens, but without encouraging a hope in the swain that he will prevail. Time is supposed to pass, leaving terrible traces of suffering—apparently to the verge of consumption—in the young man, who, on finding the girl at a well, makes his last, almost dying, appeal. He seizes her hand; but she turns away, deaf to his passionate beseeching.

In the Leech drawing the composition of Stone's picture is exactly preserved; but in place of the lady we have Sir Robert Inglis, who turns away in horror from a young gentleman of a very marked Jewish type indeed.

The present *Punch* artists have greatly the advantage of Leech, in respect of the aid derivable from photography. In these days, there is scarcely a statesman whose photograph cannot be seen in the London shop-windows, to the great advantage of the political caricaturists of to-day. It was only at the latter part of Leech's time that photography became so generally used to familiarize us with the features of our legislators, and even then I doubt if Leech took much advantage of it. He had seen all these men, and a rough sketch in his note-book, aided by his marvellous memory, was sufficient to enable him to produce unmistakable likenesses.

It remains for me to note some of the instances in which Leech's powers were brought to bear upon the social questions of the time—questions admitting of a humorous or a pathetic treatment, apart from those of a merely political character.

In 1850 a motion by Lord Ashley, afterwards Shaftesbury, was carried against the Government by a majority of ninety-three to sixty-eight, ordering that the transmission and delivery of letters on Sunday should cease in all parts of the kingdom. The new law was acted upon for some weeks, and caused so much public inconvenience, and so great and indignant a popular outcry, that the obnoxious rules were rescinded. Leech took full advantage of the opportunity thus afforded him. His ready imagination supplied him with instances in which the operation of the new law would cause loss and suffering. This was shown in a drawing which, amongst other proofs, depicts a mother in great distress because she can have no news of her sick child. And when, in September, 1850, the obnoxious regulation was withdrawn, Leech celebrated the event in an admirable cartoon, in which the promoters, Lords Russell and Ashley, dressed as Puritans, are ruefully contemplating each other, Russell addressing his fellow-Puritan with, "Verily, Brother Ashley, between you and me and the *post* we have made a nice mess of it!"

The neglect of our troops during the Crimean campaign afforded the artist many humorous and tragic subjects. The Government was accused, rightly or wrongly, of many sins of omission and commission; amongst the rest, of not providing the army with clothing suitable to the terrible winter which it was sure to have to pass in front of Sebastopol. And one of Leech's most telling drawings represents two ragged soldiers shivering in the snow. One tells the other that news has arrived of a medal that is to be awarded. "Yes," says his comrade; "but they had much better send us a coat to put it on."

Two pictures may be noted—one by Tenniel, which is infinitely pathetic, the other by Leech, ghastly in its contrast to the humorous side of the author's powers. The first represents a fashionable lady, whose magnificent ball-dress has just been fitted upon her by the dressmaker, who says:

"We would not have disappointed your ladyship at any *sacrifice*, and the robe is finished À MERVEILLE."

But the *sacrifice*! The lady turns to the looking-glass, wherein she sees the dress, and part of the cost of making it, in the appalling figure of the workwoman, whose haggard form leans back exhausted, dully lighted by a dying lamp, by the help of which all night long the lady has not been "*disappointed.*"

"The Jew and Skeleton Tailors."

The sufferings of the workers, through which their employers so often became rich, touched the tender heart of Leech, and he never lost an opportunity of pointing out the selfish tyranny of both the men and women traders who almost ground the life out of their unhappy assistants.

If John Leech could have entertained a prejudice against any human beings, it must have been against the Jewish race, for there is scarcely an instance in which he deals with the Jews that they do not suffer under his hand. The points of their physiognomy are rather cruelly prominent sometimes, even almost to caricature, and they are constantly placed in ludicrous positions. There can be no doubt that in some instances the tailor is no less a bloodsucker than the dressmaker, but I think there are as many, or more, Christian—or, rather, unchristian—tailors who "sweat" their workpeople as there are Jewish. However, in one of Leech's most powerful prints, he gives the *pas* to the Jew, who watches a group of skeleton tailors as they labour in their bones for his benefit. It is a gruesome drawing, which, once seen, can never be forgotten.

Leech was happily left to his own devices as regards the contributions to *Punch*, with the sole exception of the large cartoons, the subjects of which were always settled by the whole staff at a dinner, which took place every Wednesday. At this dinner no strangers were present. This was, and is still, the rule. Exceptions, however, were made on one or two occasions in favour of Charles Dickens, Sir Joseph Paxton, and some others.

It was, of course, open to any member to suggest a subject, and in the early Leech days it is said that the discussions on a proposed theme waxed fast and furious, Thackeray and Douglas Jerrold generally taking opposite sides. The dinners were usually held in the front room of the first-floor of No. 11, Bouverie Street—the business-place of the proprietors of the paper—and the Bedford Hotel, Covent Garden, was sometimes honoured by the presence of the staff. During the summer months the dinners took place at Greenwich, Richmond, or Blackwall; and once a year there was a more comprehensive banquet, at which compositors, readers, printers, clerks, etc., assisted. This dinner was called the "Way-goose." I am speaking of long ago. Whether these details would apply to the present time I know not.

I never knew Jerrold. I have frequently seen him, but always avoided an introduction; for, to speak the truth, I was afraid of him. I had heard so many stories of his making "dead sets" at new acquaintances as to disincline me to become one. By anybody quick at repartee I was told he was easily silenced, and an example was mentioned when a barmaid succeeded in stopping a torrent of "chaff" of which she was the victim. It appears that Jerrold went with some friends to a supper-room one night after the theatre. The supper was "topped up" with hot grog, which was served to the guests in large, old-fashioned rummers.

"There," said the girl, as she placed the big glass before Jerrold, "there's your grog, and mind you don't fall into it."

Jerrold was a very little man, and the hit told to the extent of dulling him for the rest of the evening.

At the Wednesday dinner the whole of the contents of the forthcoming number of *Punch* were discussed. When the cloth was removed and dessert laid upon the table, the first question put by the editor was:

"What shall the cartoon be?"

It is said of Tenniel that he rarely suggested a subject for the cartoon, but that the readiness with which he saw and explained the possibilities of a subject was remarkable. During the Indian Mutiny, Shirley Brooks proposed that the picture should represent the British Lion in the act of springing upon the native soldiers in revenge for the cruelties at Cawnpore. Tenniel rose to the occasion, and, as Brooks told me, he exclaimed, "By Jove, that will do for a double-page cut!" and a magnificent double-page drawing was made of it by him.

In the inevitable difference of opinion that arose on the occasion of these dinners—the chief disputants being, as I have just observed, Thackeray and Jerrold—Jerrold, being the oldest as well as the noisiest, generally came off victorious. In these rows it is said to have required all the suavity of Mark Lemon to calm the storm, his award always being final. Jerrold used to say:

"It's no use our quarrelling, for we must meet again and shake hands next Wednesday."

The last editions of the evening papers were always brought in, so that the cartoon might apply to the latest date. On the Thursday morning following the editor called at the houses of the artists to see what was being done. On Friday night all copy was delivered and put into type, and at two o'clock on Saturday proofs were revised, the forms made up, and with the last movement of the engine the whole of the type was placed under the press, which could not be moved till the Monday morning.

By means of the Wednesday meetings, the discussions arising on all questions helped both caricaturist and wit to take a broad view of things, as well as enabled the editor to get his team to draw well together and give uniformity of tone to all the contributions.

CHAPTER III.

THE LAWYER'S STORY.

By the courtesy of the proprietors of *Punch*, I am allowed to reproduce in this place a delightfully humorous drawing, the scene of which is laid in a barber's shop.

This picture explains itself, but there is a circumstance connected with it which is, I think, well worth relating; and as I heard it from Leech's own lips at one of the pleasant Egg dinners, I will give it in Leech's own words, the strangeness of the incident having left a very vivid impression on my memory. The usual company—Dickens, Forster, Lemon, etc.—was present; Leech was singing. We had listened for some time to the inevitable "King Death," when Dickens exclaimed:

"There, that will do; if you go on any longer, you will make me cry. Tell them about the lawyer who lost his client. Yes, I know the story, but they don't; and I would much rather hear it again than listen to any more of that lugubrious song."

"Well, here goes," said Leech. "I suppose there is no one at this table who neglects to improve his mind by the weekly study of *Punch*; at any rate, all civilized people are familiar with the illustrations which adorn that famous periodical. Amongst those classical works the other day was a high-art drawing by me, representing a gentleman in a barber's shop, having his hair cut. In the course of talk peculiar to his fraternity, the little hairdresser remarks that his customer's hair *is very thin on the top*. This mild observation moved the object of it, a person of irascible temper, into ungovernable fury. He springs from his chair, which he upsets in the action, and flying at the terrified barber, he exclaims, 'Confound you, you puppy! Do you think I came here to be insulted and told of my imperfections? *I'll thin your top!*'

"I'll Thin Your Top."

"Well, I don't see anything particularly facetious in the drawing, but a friend of mine, a lawyer in Bedford Row, did, and laughed whenever he thought of it. Unfortunately, the day on which the drawing was published had been fixed for a consultation upon a matter in which an old and respected client's interests were seriously involved. Legal points of extreme intricacy and difficulty were to be examined and discussed; hopes were to be encouraged, and anxiety appeased. In his information to his legal adviser, the client had arrived at a point of extreme gravity, when my unfortunate drawing obtruded itself upon the legal mind, and so disturbed it as to cause the lawyer to repress a laugh with much difficulty.

"'I see you smile,' said the client. 'Surely the very serious character of the evidence which I put before you should strike you as convin——'

"'Oh, I beg your pardon; I was not smiling.'

"'Well, you did something very like it. I really must ask for your strictest attention to facts which are capable of such absolute—— There you go again! My dear sir, what *can* there be in my statement to cause a smile? Pray think of the gravity of the case—how deeply my interests are at stake—and give me your most serious attention.'

"'I will—indeed I will,' said the lawyer, mentally devoting me and my drawing to the devil.

"For some minutes the legal gentleman succeeded in banishing the little barber and his enraged victim; but suddenly they again ruthlessly seized upon his imagination, and he laughed aloud.

"'Good God!' said the client; 'what is there to laugh at in that?'

"'I assure you, sir, I was not laughing at what you told me, which is important indeed, but at a ludicrous idea that crossed my mind.'

"'What business have ludicrous ideas in your mind when you require all its attention for business which—excuse my saying so—you are well paid for listening to?'

"The consultation proceeded; graver and graver grew the details; when, at a moment of extreme importance, the barber came again upon the scene, and the lawyer laughed loud and long.

"'It's no use; I can't get rid of it,' he said to his astonished and indignant visitor. 'There is a drawing in *Punch* to-day that is so irresistibly funny that I can't get it out of my head, and I can't help laughing whenever I think of it.'

"'I don't believe a single word you say!' said the angry client; 'and as you persist in treating my case with such insulting levity, I will go elsewhere, and endeavour to find someone who will attend to me. And as for you, sir, I will never trouble you again on this or any other matter.'

"That," said Leech, "is how my friend lost his client."

CHAPTER IV.

LOVE OF FIELD SPORTS.

Leech had long passed his boyish days before his love for field sports showed itself in his works. I recollect his saying how fruitful of subject the hunting-field, the stubble, and the stream would prove to the artist who was also a sportsman. In his early works, dealing as they did chiefly with the London life of the street or the home, we find the horse playing an inferior part; and it was not till he felt the importance of varying his subjects, and of supplying the public with the sporting scenes they love so much, that, mounted by his friend Adams, he joined the "Puckeridge" and became one of the "field."

Leech was a timid rider. He much preferred an open gate to a thickset hedge, and the highroad to either. He must, however, have frequently been in full career with the "field"; how otherwise could he have acquired his knowledge of the thorough sportsman's seat on horseback, the cut of his clothes—correct even to the number of buttons—and, above all, display that Heaven-gifted power of showing the horse in repose, as well as in all the varieties of action? Landseer and all the animal-painters within my knowledge studied the horse from casts, often from the Elgin marbles, before they attempted drawing from the living animal. Landseer made himself acquainted with the superficial structure by dissection; but Leech, without any preparatory study whatever, drew the hunter, the cab-horse, the hackney, the rough pony, the cob—no matter which—in absolute perfection.

"Give Her Her Head, Jack."

In the autograph letters which, through Mr. Adams' kindness, I am permitted to publish, Leech's constant charge to his friend to get him a horse suitable to a "timid, elderly gentleman," or to give the animal some preliminary gallops himself so as to take the *freshness* out of him, prove, as I said before, that Leech was anything but a daring rider. In spite of his care, however, he had some ugly falls, in which, happily, his hat was the greatest sufferer. Numbers of the hunting scenes were *facts*, and the persons represented were Leech and his friend—notably one in which the artist is riding a mare afflicted with the "freshness" he dreaded, which his friend observing, shouts, "Give her her head, Jack! give her her head!" while it is pretty evident that more "head" will lead to the rider being swept from the saddle by the branches through which the mare is plunging.

> "Barlow, Derbyshire,
> "July, 1852.

"My dear Charley,

"You will see from the above address that I am still rusticating. I expect to be in town soon after the 12th of August, and then, after I have done my month's work, I am your man. You say when, and, if you are quite sure it will not distress Mrs. Adams, I will bring my wife with me. Charles Eaton [Mrs. Leech's brother] says he will come too. I am sure nothing would please him more than to run down to Barkway. Don't make yourself uncomfortable about the quantity of sport. I shall be quite satisfied with what you offer me. I rejoice to hear such good accounts of your wife and little ones. Pray give our united regards to her and them, and believe me ever,

"Yours faithfully,
"JOHN LEECH."

"OH, IF THIS IS ONE OF THE PLACES CHARLEY SPOKE OF, I SHALL GO BACK!"

Yet another fact. Somewhere in the Puckeridge country there is a deep gully, or dried-up watercourse, with precipitous sides, with which Leech, one hunting-morning, found himself face to face. Some of the "field" had crossed, and were climbing the opposite bank. Leech pulled up, and said to his friend:

"Oh, if this is one of the places Charley spoke of, I shall go back!"

I am able here to give the rough sketch, now in Mr. Adams' possession, from which the drawing was taken that afterwards appeared in *Punch*.

Some years ago I took my exercise chiefly on horseback, and, after risking my neck several times from the "freshness" of a thoroughbred mare, I thought it best to get rid of her. Amongst the rest of my horsey friends, I thought Leech would be likely to know of an animal that might suit me, and I spoke to him on the subject. Leech soon succeeded, and sent the horse for my inspection. The man who brought the animal for approval assured me that a child could ride him with perfect safety. I liked his looks, and bought him. My first and last ride upon my new purchase was to Rotten Row in the height of the season. Whether he was a horse of Radical or Socialistic principles, or not, I cannot say; but what I soon discovered was a determined dislike to the aristocratic company in which he found himself; he shied at the ladies and kicked at the gentlemen, and finally took to what is called "buck-jumping," an amusement which would speedily have relieved him of my company if I had not taken advantage of a momentary cessation of his antics and safely descended from his detestable back. Leech soon heard of "the dangers I had passed," when he wrote to me as follows:

"6, The Terrace, Kensington,
"Sunday.

"My dear Frith,

"I was shocked last night at the Garrick to hear from Elmore that I had nearly killed you through recommending a horse which had misbehaved himself in the Park. To be sure, I told you that I had been to look at an animal for my little girl, and that it did not suit, and I told you that it might be worth your looking at, as I had heard that it was young, sound, and steady; but if you ride a beast that you know nothing about in Rotten Row, and if that beast has not been out for a week, or probably a fortnight, I must protest against being made answerable for the consequences. I most sincerely hope, however, that you are not hurt or come to grief in any way.

"Believe me,
"Yours always,
"John Leech."

It goes without saying that so true-hearted a man as John Leech, would be—as indeed he was—a model of the domestic virtues—the best of husbands and fathers, and a most dutiful and affectionate son. In evidence of the latter, I put before my readers some letters written to his parents in his maturer years, which will amply justify what I say of him.

"32, Brunswick Square,
"February 25, 1854.

"My dear Papa,

"I am sure you will be glad to hear that you have a little granddaughter.

"She came into the world at a quarter-past eleven o'clock—just now—and she is, with dear Annie (to me a *novel* phrase), 'as well as can be expected.'

"Kind love to all.

"Your affectionate son
"JOHN.

"Tell Polly that the flag will be hoisted!"

"8, St. Nicholas Cliff, Scarboro',
"August 30, 1858.

"MY DEAR MAMMA,

"Thank you with my best love for thinking of my birthday. I hope you will be able to wish me happy returns of the day for many and many a year to come. The children gave your kisses very heartily, I assure you. You will be glad to hear, I am sure, that they were never better.

"Thank God they are thriving beautifully, which is a great happiness to me. I wish you could see them making dirt pies and gardens on the sands. A great many people notice them—indeed, although I say it, between you and me, I don't see any nicer little folks down here. If either you or papa could come here for a time we would endeavour to take the best care of you. I am no great hand at pen-and-inking, as you know, so you will excuse a very short note. I thought, however, that you would like to know that I got from Ireland safe and sound, and always believe me,

"My dear mamma,
"Your affectionate son,
"JOHN."

"1, Crescent, Scarboro',
"August 29, 1859.

"MY DEAR MAMMA,

"It would be a great comfort to me, and I think it would be pleasant for you, if you would come here and see us for as long as you can spare the time. I want very much to go into the north, but I do not like leaving Annie quite alone with the chicks. We can give you a bed in, I think you will say, a tolerably comfortable house. Come as soon as you can, and stay as long as you can. I think it would do you good; only bring warm things, as when it is cold here, it is very cold. By the way, it is my birthday. What shall I say? Well, I wish you many happy returns of the day, and believe me, with best love from all to all,

"Your affectionate son,
"JOHN."

"5, Pleydell Gardens,
"Sandgate Road, Folkestone,
"August 29, 1862.

"MY DEAR MAMMA,

"Many thanks for your note this morning. You will be glad to know, I am sure, that it found us all very well. May you be able to send me such a congratulation for many a year to come. And with best love to you, and to all at home, believe me ever,

"Your affectionate son,
"JOHN.

"Tell papa that if he would like to run down here, we can give him a bed. He would like to see a couple of little brown faces. I am going away for a few days (on Monday, I think); so if any of you could keep Annie with the chicks, and keep her company while I am absent, it would be very nice, I think."

A great deal has been said—and with a certain amount of truth, no doubt—about the difference between a drawing on wood as it leaves the hands of the artist, and as it appears after its sufferings at the hands of the wood-engraver. Leech is reported to have replied to an admiring friend, who was extolling one of his drawings:

"Ah, wait till you see what it looks like in *Punch* next week."

I once saw one of Leech's drawings on the wood, and I afterwards saw it in *Punch*, and I remember wondering at the fidelity with which it was rendered. Some of the lines, finer than the finest hair, had been cut away or *thickened*, but the character, the vigour, and the beauty were scarcely damaged. To Mr.

Swain, who for many years cut all Leech's drawings, the artist owed and acknowledged obligation; he thought himself fortunate in avoiding certain other wood-cutters, who were somewhat remorseless in their operations.

Mr. Swain, the wood-engraver, writes:

"For twenty-five years I engraved nearly all Mr. Leech's drawings. I always found him kind, and willing to forgive any of my shortcomings in not rendering his touches in all things. My work was always against time. I seldom had more time than two days to engrave one of his drawings in.

"Photographing drawings on wood was not known in his time, or it would have been a great advantage to him; instead of drawing on the block, he would then have drawn on paper, as most artists do in the present day, and had his drawings photographed on the wood, thus preserving the finished drawings, which would have been of great value now; besides, it would have been a great help to the engraver, always to have the original drawing to refer to in engraving the blocks.

"He never had any models, and rarely ever made any sketches. He showed me a little note-book once with a few thumb-nail sketches of bits of background, but he seemed never to forget anything he saw, and could always go back in his memory for any little bit of country street he might want for background, etc.

"It was generally very late in the week before he could get his drawings ready, which gave very little time to the engraver to do justice to his work.

"His first introduction to *Punch* was through Mr. Percival Leigh.

"Mr. Leech was a man of very nervous temperament. I will give you an instance of this. Mr. Mark Lemon told me one day that Leech had been invited to a gentleman's house in the country for a few days' hunting. He arrived there in the evening. He was awakened early in the morning by a grating noise made by the gardener rolling the gravel under his window —noise he could never endure. This had such an effect upon his nerves, that he got up, packed his things, and was off to town before any of the family were aware of it. A barrel-organ was to him an instrument of torture.

"He had lived in Russell Square for many years, but for some time before his death he took a large house—6, The Terrace, Kensington.

"I remember going to see him at his new house. He took great delight in showing me over it, and pointing out that he had had double windows put in all over the house *to keep all noises out.*"

CHAPTER V.

INVENTORS AND ILLUSTRATORS.

In looking at the plethora of lovely women's faces in the "Pictures of Life and Character," the spectator may fairly ask himself to realize, if he can, anything more exquisite; and if he fail, he will also fail to imagine that the charming creatures could have suffered much in their passage from the wood to the paper.

I have said elsewhere that Charles Dickens was an occasional guest at the *Punch* Wednesday dinners; he was also an intimate friend of several of the writers, notably of Leech, Lemon, and Douglas Jerrold. Dickens was, of course, one of Thackeray's warmest admirers, but I am pretty sure that the friendship between those great men could never have reached intimacy. Though Leech failed in his application for the post of illustrator of the "Pickwick Papers," he showed himself to be at one with the great writer in the etchings and woodcuts with which he ornamented Dickens' Christmas books, in conjunction with Stanfield, Maclise, Cattermole, and others. Though Leech's etchings are inferior as works of art to his wood-drawings, they still show the same beauty, and perfect realization of character; in this assertion I am borne out by the illustrations in the "Christmas Carol," and by those in the "Haunted Man and the Battle of Life."

In my own profession I have observed, almost as a rule, that the artist who habitually invents his own subjects—in other words, draws upon himself for original ideas—generally fails, comparatively, in his attempts to realize the ideas of others. May I not say the same of many writers? Dickens, for instance, wrote of the life about him; but if, like Scott, he had attempted to revive the past, would he have produced work worthy to rank with "David Copperfield"? Scott seems to me a still more conspicuous supporter of my theory, for he tried modern life in "St. Ronan's Well," and produced a book incontestably inferior to "Kenilworth."

Our historical painters have almost invariably failed in their attempts upon everyday life; this extends even to the painters of *genre*. Witness the works of the elder Leslie, who painted scenes from Shakespeare, Molière, and the poets of the last century, with a success that would have delighted the authors; but when he sought inspiration from the life about him, the result was far from satisfactory—conspicuous, indeed, in its contrast with his perfect rendering, of "Sir Roger de Coverley" or "Uncle Toby," and the alluring "Widow Wadman."

But the greatest of English painters is the greatest help to me in the contention into which I venture to enter. Hogarth was beguiled by a spirit, which must have been evil, into painting huge Scripture subjects. The *size* of these pictures, always of the proportion of full life, was unsuited to his hand, while the themes became ludicrous under his treatment. He failed completely also as an illustrator, witness his designs from "Hudibras." In the Bristol Gallery, and in the Foundling Hospital, these specimens of perverted genius may be seen; and no one can look at them without regret that time should have been so misspent—time which might have given us another immortal series like the "Marriage à la Mode."

JACK JOHNSON'S ATTEMPT TO RESCUE DERVAL.

I fancy I can hear my readers say—And what has all this to do with John Leech? Well, this: Leech is now about to pose as the destroyer, in his own person, of my theory—he is, in fact, the exception to my rule; for though the incidents in Albert Smith's "Ledbury" and "Brinvilliers" bear no comparison

31

in human interest with the delightful transcripts of real life to be found in such profusion in the pictures of "Life and Character," Leech's rendering of them could not be surpassed.

The tragic and humorous powers of the artist are fully displayed in the examples which follow. In the first, from "Ledbury," "Jack Johnson attempts to rescue Derval": the awful swirl of the river as it engulfs the drowning man, while his would-be rescuer, finding the stream too strong for him, clings frantically to a ring in the stonework of the bridge, a full moon lightning up the scene, and throwing the Pont Neuf which spans the Seine in the distance into deep shadow—all are combined with admirable skill into, perhaps, the most powerful etching and the most perfect illustration in the book.

In the second example the artist is in full sympathy with his author—"Mrs. De Robinson holds a Conversazione of Talented People;" and amongst them is "the foreign gentleman who executes an air upon the grand piano." Here we have Leech using the scene as a peg upon which he can hang the humorous character in which he takes such hearty, healthy delight. The performer himself is scarcely a caricature of the foreign pianist; while his audience, not forgetting the deaf old lady in the corner—includes the affected gentleman, whose soul is in Elysium; together with a variety of types, in which "lovely woman" is not forgotten.

CHAPTER VI.

"INGOLDSBY LEGENDS."

In the "Ingoldsby Legends" Leech found a very congenial field for the exercise of his powers. Though I will not presume to prophesy respecting literary merit, I venture to think that, during the course of his practice, Leech's illustrations have occasionally appeared attached to literature scarcely worthy of them; they will, doubtless, in some cases, act as the salt, which will preserve for posterity certain books of an ephemeral character. This remark cannot apply to the "Ingoldsby Legends," which is a work that "the world will not willingly let die," until delightful wit and humour, wedded to no less delightful verse, cease to charm. The burden of the illustrations of the "Legends" falls upon the worthy shoulders of John Tenniel, and they show some of the strongest work of that admirable artist. Leech appears in diminished force as to numbers, but in the examples I give he leaves nothing to wish for.

> "For, only see there! in the midst of the Square,
> Where, perch'd upon poles six feet high in the air,
> Sit, chained to the stake, some two, three, or four pair
> Of wretches, whose eyes, nose, complexion, and hair
> Their Jewish descent but too plainly declare;
> Each clothed in a garment more frightful by far, a
> Smock-frock sort of gaberdine called a *Samarra*,
> With three times the number of devils upon it—
> A proportion observed on the sugar-loaf bonnet;
> With this further distinction, of mischief a proof,
> That every fiend-Jack stands upright on his hoof!
> While the picture flames, spread over body and head,
> Are three times as crooked, and three times as red!
> All, too, pointing upwards, as much as to say,
> 'Here's the real *bonne-bouche* of the Auto da Fé!'
>
> "Torquemada, meanwhile, with his cold, cruel smile,
> Sits looking on calmly, and watching the pile,
> As his hooded 'Familiars' (their names, as some tell, come
> From their being so much more 'familiar' than 'welcome')
> Have by this begun to be 'poking their fun,'
> And their fire-brands, as if they were so many posies
> Of lilies and roses, up to the noses

33

Of Lazarus Levi and Moses Ben Moses,
And similar treatment is forcing out hollow moans
From Aby Ben Lasco and Ikey Ben Solomons,
Whose beards—this a black, that inclining to grizzle—
Are smoking and curling, and all in a frizzle;
The King, at the same time, his Dons and his Visitors,
Sit, sporting smiles, like the Holy Inquisitors!"

"16, Lansdowne Place, Brighton,
"September 3, 1863.

"MY DEAR SIR,

"I have been obliged to make the 'Auto da Fé' this size, as I found I
could not possibly get the subject on to a small block. You will see, too,
that I have altered the appearance of the victims. It occurred to me that a
real human being burning alive was hardly fun, so I have made them a
set of Guy Fawkeses, and added, I hope, to the humour while getting rid
of the horror.

"Believe me, my dear Sir,
"Yours faithfully,
"JOHN LEECH.

"RICHARD BENTLEY, ESQ."

In the second example we have the figure of a maid at a well, which Leech
has given us with the charm that never fails him. Her astonishment at the head
in the bucket might have been indicated more forcibly, but there, I fancy, the
engraver must have been to blame; yet he gives the head of Gengulphus with
such perfection of expression and character as to make one feel that the
original drawing of it could scarcely have been better.

A LAY OF ST. GENGULPHUS.

"But scarce had she given the windlass a twirl,
    'Ere Gengulphus's head, from the well's bottom said,
In mild accents, 'Do help us out, that's a good girl!'

THE MAID AND THE HEAD OF GENGULPHUS.

"Only fancy her dread when she saw a great head
    In her bucket—with fright she was ready to drop!
Conceive, if you can, how she roared and she ran,
    With the head rolling after her, bawling out 'Stop!'"

As this memoir progresses I propose to submit further illustrations from some of the many serials, novels, tales, poems, etc., with which Leech was connected. I also propose, in the course of my narrative, to quote opinions of Leech's powers from men better qualified to judge of them, and able to express their opinions in far more felicitous language than mine. Amongst those Dickens takes a foremost place. I think the friendship between Leech and Dickens began very early in the life of the former; the nature of Leech's work, and the modest and gentle character of the man, were especially attractive to Dickens.

In the amateur company of actors formed by Dickens, Leech was a conspicuous figure; but his heart was not in the work, though he entirely sympathized with the object of it, which was of a charitable nature, resulting in many performances—very successful in a pecuniary sense—for the benefit of poor and deserving literary men. The company consisted of Dickens, Mark

Lemon, John Forster, G. H. Lewis, Douglas Jerrold, Leech, Egg, Wilkie Collins, Frank Stone, and others, who christened themselves "The Guild of Literature and Art." The late Lord Lytton took great interest in the Guild, for which he wrote a play called "Not so Bad as We Seem; or, Many Sides to a Character," and to this he added a gift of land on his estate in Hertfordshire, where some houses of a superior cottage form were built, in which decayed artists and authors were to end their days; but these gentlemen declined to *begin* any days there under the conditions prescribed; and when the houses were built, tenants for them could not be found. The Guild, therefore, was something of a fiasco, with the exception of the relief it afforded in several instances to worthy objects.

Leech acted in the first play that the amateurs ventured upon, no less than Ben Jonson's "Every Man in his Humour," in which Dickens played Bobadil and Leech Master Matthew. This occurred about 1847, I think, and I was honoured by an invitation to the first or second performance. *Par parenthèse*, I may add that I had the honour of being asked to join the company, but feeling that I could not learn a part, or, if I did get over that difficulty, the footlights would paralyze my memory, and also having neither face nor figure for the stage, I thought it best to "stick to my last."

Though Leech had a good part in "Every Man," strange to say, I have no recollection of his performance; though that of Dickens, Jerrold, Egg, and others remains vividly in my memory. Dickens gave proofs in Bobadil, and in many other characters, that he might have been a great actor. The same, nor anything like it, could not be said with truth of Leech, if he played his other parts no better than he did that of Slender in the "Merry Wives of Windsor." It is only in that character that I can remember him, though I must have seen him in others. The tone in which he said "Oh, sweet Anne Page!" can I ever forget? There was a ring of impatience in his performance, a kind of "Oh, I wish this was all over!" that was plainly perceptible to those who knew him intimately. Leech's tall figure and handsome face told well upon the stage, but with those his attractions as an actor ceased. In Lord Lytton's play Leech had no part, I think, but my old friend Egg played that of a poor poet, who is discovered in a miserable attic when the curtain rises, and the poet soliloquizes to the effect that "Years ago, when under happier circumstances"—something or other. Egg always begun, "Here's a go, when under," etc. Unlike Leech, Egg was fond of acting, but, like Leech, he displayed no capacity for the art.

CHAPTER VII.

DICKENS AND THACKERAY ON LEECH.

Perhaps the most striking difference between Leech and the caricaturists who preceded him, as well as those who were his contemporaries, was shown in the part that beauty played in every drawing in which it could be appropriately introduced; he may be credited with the creation of many of the loveliest creatures that ever fell from the pencil of an artist. Leech revelled in beauty as Gillray and Rowlandson revelled in ugliness.

In 1841 a work appeared, in book-form, of sketches by Leech, entitled "The Rising Generation," in which the rising youth, with their mannish manners, were satirized. Of this book Dickens wrote:

"We enter our protest against those of the rising generation who are precociously in love being made the subject of merriment by a pitiless and unsympathizing world. We never saw a boy more distinctly in the right than the young gentleman kneeling in the chair to beg a lock of hair from his pretty cousin to take back to school. Madness is in her apron, and Virgil, dog-eared and defaced, is in her ringlets. Doubts may suggest themselves of the perfect disinterestedness of the other young gentleman contemplating the fair girl at the piano—doubts engendered by his worldly allusion to 'tin,' although that may have arisen in his modest consciousness of his own inability to support an establishment; but that he should be 'deucedly inclined to go and cut that fellow out' appears to us one of the most natural emotions of the human breast. The young gentleman with the dishevelled hair and clasped hands, who loves the transcendent beauty with the bouquet and can't be happy without her, is to us a withering and desolate spectacle. Who *could* be happy without her? The growing youths are not less happily observed and depicted than the grown women. The languid little creature, who 'hasn't danced since he was quite a boy,' is perfect; and the eagerness of the small dancer, whom he declines to receive for a partner at the hands of the glorious old lady of the house (the little feet quite ready for the first position, the whole heart projected into the quadrille, and the glance peeping timidly at the desired one out of a flutter of hope and doubt), is quite delightful to look at. The intellectual youth, who awakens the tremendous wrath of a Norma of private life by considering woman an inferior animal, is lecturing at the present moment, we understand, on the Concrete in connection with the Will. The legs of the young philosopher who considers Shakespeare an overrated man were seen by us dangling over the side of an omnibus last Tuesday. We have no acquaintance with the scowling young gentleman, who is clear that 'if his governor don't like the way he is going on, why, he must have chambers and so much a week;' but, if he is not by this time in Van Diemen's Land, he will certainly go to it through Newgate. We should exceedingly dislike to have personal property in a strong-box, to live in the quiet suburb of Camberwell, and to be in the relation of bachelor uncle to that youth. In all his designs, whatever Mr. Leech desires to do he does. His drawing seems to us charming, and the expression, indicated by the simplest means, is exactly the natural expression, and is recognised as such at once. Some forms of our existing life will never have a better chronicler. His wit is good-natured, and always the wit of a gentleman. He has a becoming sense of responsibility and restraint; he delights in agreeable things, and he imparts some pleasant air of his own to things not pleasant in themselves; he is suggestive and full of matter, and he is always improving. Into the tone as well as into the execution of what he does, he has brought a certain elegance which is altogether new, without involving any compromise of what is true. Popular art in England has not had so rich an acquisition."

In the endeavour to satisfy Dickens with the type required for the characters in his stories, Leech encountered the difficulty that all the author's illustrators had to master. "Phiz" made many drawings in Dickens' presence before he could realize the author's idea of Mr. Dombey; Cruikshank was more than once required to redraw a whole scene from "Oliver Twist"; and Leech has often been heard to speak of the minute details as to feature, height, thinness or fatness—in fact, every physical and, so far as it could be shown by appearance, mental quality—that Dickens insisted upon before he could be satisfied with the *vera effigies* of one of his characters. The feelings of the great author, then, may be imagined when he found—too late for correction— a terrible error into which Leech had fallen in the drawing of a scene from "The Battle of Life," by introducing a personage into a scene which closes the second part of the tale, who was not intended to have been present.

It was in December, 1846, that "The Battle of Life" made one of the series of Christmas stories. In Leech's unfortunate illustration, which represented the flight of the bride, he made the mistake of supposing that Michael Warden had taken part in the elopement, and introduced his figure with that of Marian. Leech's error was not discovered until too late for remedy, the publication of the book having been delayed to the utmost limit expressly for those drawings; and it is highly characteristic of Dickens, and of the true regard he had for the artist, that, knowing the pain he must inflict, under the circumstances, by complaining, he never reproached Leech; excusing him, no doubt, on the ground of the hurry and confusion under which so much of his work was produced; but anyone who reads the story carefully will see what

38

havoc the mistake makes of one of the most delicate turns in it.

Dickens wrote thus to Forster in reference to the grievous error: "When I first saw it, it was with a horror and agony not to be expressed. Of course, I need not tell *you*, my dear fellow, that Warden had no business in the elopement scene; he was never there. In the first hot sweat of this surprise and novelty, I was going to implore that the printing of that sheet might be stopped, and the figure taken out of the block; but when I thought of the pain this might give to our kind-hearted Leech, and that what is such a monstrous enormity to me as never entered my brain, may not so present itself to others, I became more composed, though the fact is wonderful to me. No doubt a great number of copies will be printed by the time this reaches you, and therefore I shall take it for granted that it stands as it is. Leech otherwise is very good, and the illustrations altogether are by far the best that have been done for any of my Christmas books."

It may appear presumptuous in me to differ from Dickens in respect to the illustrations to "The Battle of Life"; but, in my opinion, these are not to be compared favourably with those of the "Christmas Carol." With the well-known readiness of people to ferret out mistakes, it seems strange that the illustrator's mistake was never publicly noticed.

The first series of "The Pictures of Life and Character," reprinted from *Punch*, appeared in 1854. They were heartily welcomed by the public; and it is as follows that Thackeray, Leech's intimate friend, speaks of them in the *Quarterly Review*, in an article published at that time:

"This book is better than plum-cake at Christmas. It is one enduring plum-cake, which you may eat, and which you may slice and deliver to your friends, and to which, having cut it, you may come again, and welcome, from year's end to year's end. In the frontispiece you see Mr. Punch examining the pictures in his gallery—a portly, well-dressed, middle-aged, respectable gentleman, in a white neck-cloth and a polite evening costume, smiling in a very bland and agreeable manner upon one of his pleasant drawings, taken out of one of his handsome portfolios. Mr. Punch has very good reason to smile at the work and be satisfied with the artist. Mr. Leech, his chief contributor, and some hundred humorists, with pencil and pen, have served Mr. Punch admirably. There is no blinking the fact that in Mr. Punch's cabinet John Leech is the right-hand man.

"Fancy a number of *Punch* without John Leech's pictures! What would you give for it? The learned gentlemen who wrote the book must feel that without him it were as well left alone. Look at the rivals whom the popularity of *Punch* has brought into the field—the direct imitators of Mr. Leech's manner —the artists with a manner of their own. How inferior their pencils are to his humour in depicting the public manners, in arresting and amusing the nation! The truth, the strength, the free vigour, the kind humour, the John Bull pluck and spirit of that hand are approached by no competitor. With what dexterity he draws a horse, a woman, a child! He feels them all, so to speak, like a man. What plump young beauties those are with which Mr. Punch's chief contributor supplies the old gentleman's pictorial harem! What famous thews and sinews Mr. Punch's horses have, and how Briggs on the back of them scampers across the country! You see youth, strength, enjoyment, manliness, in those drawings, and in none more so, to our thinking, than in the hundred pictures of children which this artist loves to design. Like a brave, hearty, good-natured Briton, he becomes quite soft and tender with the little creatures, pats gently their little golden heads, and watches with unfailing pleasure their ways, their jokes, laughter, caresses. *Enfants terribles* come home from Eton, young miss practising her first flirtation, poor little ragged Polly making dirt-pies in the gutter, or staggering under the weight of her nurse-child, who is as big as herself—all these little ones, patrician and plebeian, meet with kindness from this kind heart, and are watched with curious anxiety by this amiable observer.

"Now, anyone who looks over Mr. Leech's portfolio must see that the social pictures which he gives us are authentic. What comfortable little drawing-rooms and dining-rooms, what snug libraries, we enter! What fine young gentlemanly wags they are, those beautiful little dandies, who wake up gouty old grandpapa to ring the bell; who decline aunt's pudding and custards, saying that they will reserve themselves for anchovy-toast with the claret; who talk together behind ball-room doors, where Fred whispers Charley, pointing to a dear little partner seven years old, 'My dear Charley, she has very much gone off; you should have seen that girl last season!'

"Look well at the economy of the famous Mr. Briggs. How snug, quiet, and appropriate all the appointments are! What a comfortable, neat, clean, middle-class house Briggs' is (in the Bayswater suburb of London, we should guess from the sketches of the surrounding scenery)! What a good stable he has, with a loose-box for those celebrated hunters which he rides! How pleasant, clean, and warm his breakfast-table looks! What a trim maid brings in the boots that horrify Mrs. B.! What a snug dressing-room he has, complete in all its appointments, and in which he appears trying on that delightful hunting-cap which Mrs. Briggs flings into the fire! How cosy all the Briggs party seem in their drawing-room, Briggs reading a treatise on dog-breaking by a lamp, mamma and grannie with their respective needlework, the children clustering round a big book of prints—a great book of prints such as this before us, at this season, must make thousands of children happy by as many firesides! The inner life of all these people is represented. Leech draws them as naturally as Teniers depicts Dutch boors, or Morland pigs and stables. It is your house and mine; we are looking at everybody's family circle. Our boys, coming from school, give themselves such airs, the young scapegraces! Our girls, going to parties, are so tricked out by fond mammas—a social history of London in the middle of the nineteenth century. As such future students—lucky they to have a book so pleasant!—will regard these pages; even the mutations of fashion they may follow here, if they be so inclined. Mr. Leech has as fine an eye for tailory and millinery as for horseflesh. How they change, these cloaks and bonnets! How we have to pay milliners' bills from year to year! Where are those prodigious *chatelaines* of 1850, which no lady could be without? Where are those charming waistcoats, those *stunning* waistcoats, which our young girls used to wear a few seasons back, and which caused 'Gus, in the sweet little sketch of 'La Mode,' to ask Ellen for her tailor's address? 'Gus is a young warrior by this time, very likely facing the enemy at Inkerman; and pretty Ellen, and that love of a sister of hers, are married and happy, let us hope, superintending one of those delightful nursery scenes which our artist depicts with such tender humour. Fortunate artist, indeed! You see he must have been bred at a good public school, and that he has ridden many a good horse in his day; paid, no doubt out of his own pocket, for the originals of those lovely caps and bonnets; and watched paternally the ways, smiles, frolics, and slumbers of his favourite little people.

"As you look at the drawings, secrets come out of them—private jokes, as it were, imparted to you by the author for your special delectation. How remarkably, for instance, has Mr. Leech observed the hairdressers of the present age! Mr. Tongs, whom that hideous old bald woman who ties on her bonnet at the glass informs that 'she has used the whole bottle of Balm of California, but her hair comes off yet'—you can see the bears' grease not only on Tongs' head, but on his hands, which he is clapping clammily together. Remark him who is telling his client 'there is cholera in the hair,' and that lucky rogue whom that young lady bids to cut off a long thick piece—for somebody, doubtless. All these men are different and delightfully natural and absurd. Why should hairdressing be an absurd profession?

"The amateur will remark what an excellent part hands play in Mr. Leech's pieces; his admirable actors use them with perfect naturalness. Look at Betty putting down the urn; at cook laying her hands upon the kitchen-table, whilst the policeman grumbles at the cold meat. They are cooks' and housemaids' hands without mistake, and not without a certain beauty, too. That bald old lady tying on her bonnet at Tongs' has hands which you see are trembling. Watch the fingers of the two old harridans who are talking scandal; for what long years they have pointed out holes in their neighbours' dresses and mud on their flounces!

"'Here's a go! I've lost my diamond ring!'

"As the dustman utters this pathetic cry and looks at his hands, you burst out laughing. These are among the little points of humour. One could indicate hundreds of such as one turns over the pleasant pages.

"There is a little snob, or gent, whom we all of us know, who wears little tufts on his little chin, outrageous pins and pantaloons, smokes cigars on tobacconists' counters, sucks his cane in the streets, struts about with Mrs. Snob and the baby (the latter an immense woman, whom Snob nevertheless bullies), who is a favourite abomination of Leech, and pursued by that savage humourist into a thousand of his haunts. There he is choosing at the tailor's—such waistcoats! Yonder he is giving a shilling to the sweeper who calls him 'Capting.' Now he is offering a paletot to a huge giant who is going out in the rain. They don't know their own pictures very likely; if they did, they would have a meeting, and thirty or forty of them would be deputed to thrash Mr. Leech. One feels a pity for the poor little bucks.

"Just one word to the unwary specially to note the backgrounds of landscapes in Leech's drawings—homely drawings of moor and wood and sea-shore and London street—the scenes of his little dramas. They are as excellently true to nature as the actors themselves. Our respect for the genius and humour which invented both increases as we look and look again at the designs. May we have more of them—more pleasant Christmas volumes over which we and our children may laugh together! Can we have too much of truth and fun and beauty and kindness?"

In this delightfully appreciative spirit wrote Thackeray—a man of profounder genius than Leech—of his friend's work. It is said that when he was asked to name the most intimate and dearest friend of his life, Thackeray replied, "John Leech."

CHAPTER VIII.

DEAN HOLE.

In 1858 a second series of "Pictures of Life and Character," and later a third, were presented to a delighted public. The history of the immortal Briggs, collected from *Punch's* pages, was also published in separate form. In this year Leech made the acquaintance of the Rev. S. Reynolds Hole, now Dean of Rochester, a kindred spirit, whose admiration of the artist's work had long created a burning desire for his personal acquaintance. It was upon Easter Monday that the first meeting took place, and thus Mr. Hole describes very correctly Leech's appearance:

"Well, he was very like my idea of him, only 'more so.' A slim, elegant figure, over six feet in height, with a grand head, on which nature had written 'gentleman'—with wonderful genius in his ample forehead; wonderful penetration, observation, humour, in his blue-gray Irish eyes; and wonderful sweetness, sympathy and mirth about his lips, which seemed to speak in silence."

These words bring my old friend again before me, but I think Mr. Hole fails to notice the slight shadow of melancholy that was never long absent from his handsome face. Mr. Hole says that, vividly as the first interview comes back to him, he can recall but little of the conversation. It appears Leech had been out with the hounds on this special Monday, in company with his friend Adams, in the Belvoir country, where his presence soon became known to the "field"; and Leech as speedily discovered, by the whisperings among the sportsmen, that he was expected to perform acts of horsemanship which would throw those of "Herne the Hunter" into insignificance. "He being the quietest and most retiring of riders, much as he loved the sport, and never going over a fence if he could find a gap or a gate, it seemed, nevertheless, to be the general impression and belief of the yeomen who followed his Grace of Rutland's hounds that when a fox was found the celebrated Mr. Leech would utter a wild Irish yell, clench his teeth, put both spurs into his steed, and bound over the country like a mad buck. His complete inaptitude for these gymnastics, and the consequent disgust and disappointment of the agricultural interest when he made early deviation from the chase in favour of the King's highway, seemed to please him vastly."

Mr. Hole also speaks enthusiastically of his first meeting Thackeray at a dinner at Leech's, when he and Thackeray stood up together, like Thornhill and Olivia in the "Vicar of Wakefield," to see which was the taller. Mr. Hole won the day by proving himself to be two inches "longer" than Thackeray, who was six feet two, the longer gentleman being six feet four.

The story of Thackeray and a very tall friend going to see a giant, and being asked by the man at the door of the exhibition if they "were in the business," I have heard told differently. My friend Alfred Elmore, R.A., who was intimate with Thackeray, in speaking of that great writer's personal appearance (which, never prepossessing, had been injured by a broken nose acquired in the same way as that misfortune happened to Michael Angelo), told me that he—Thackeray—was passing by an exhibition of a giant, when the humour took him to ask the man at the door if he was in want of a giant.

"Well," said the man, "yes, we do; but not such a d——d ugly one as you."

"John Leech's consideration for others," says Mr. Hole, "was patent wherever he went; but his anxiety for his friends and their enjoyment and amusement in his own house was a very winsome sight to see…. Far too much of a gentleman to be a gourmand, though he was wont to say he deserved a good dinner when he had done a hard day's work, and that, as a matter of economy, he was reluctantly compelled to eat and drink of the best lest he should injure his manipulation, he seemed to think, nevertheless, that his guests were bound to be greedy, and that it was his duty to provide the material. I remember that on one occasion the strawberries were so large that he put the largest on a plate and handed it to a servant, with a request that it might be carved on the sideboard."

Mr. Hole gives a charming picture of Leech and himself in the sunny glades of Sherwood Forest. After lamenting that the country might be dull to the artist with only his friend's company to amuse him, and expressing his anxiety on the subject, he says:

"I soon saw that my anxiety was foolish. It was evidently, as he said, a grand enjoyment to him simply to sit under a tree and rest; to hear the throstle instead of the hurdy-gurdy; to see the sun instead of the smoke…. He could only sigh his admiration. Presently he opened his pocket sketch-book, and put a point to his pencil; but he turned from one bit of loveliness to another as he sauntered on, and soon closed his book in a kind of profound but calm resignation. 'Much too beautiful for work,' he said; 'I can do no work to-day.' So we sat among the bracken, and drank that delicious air…."

Mr. Hole was, and perhaps still is, a great rose-grower; and the day after the forest walk he gave a garden-party in honour of Leech and the roses. The roses, it appears, were not only brilliant in their summer glory on their native trees, but also glorious indeed on the faces of the young ladies who fluttered about Leech, "with evident expectation of having their portraits taken, for the

I am indebted to one of his Charterhouse schoolfellows, a very young old gentleman indeed. Mr. Charles Maitland Tate's name may be found in the first division of the fourth form in the list of scholars of 1828. Mr. Maitland's first acquaintance with "little Johnny Leech" began at Brighton in 1823, where he found our embryo six-year-old artist learning equestrian accomplishments, with the help of a small pony and the instruction of "an old retired jockey," who was one of the stable servants of George IV. at the Pavilion.

"Leech was a gentle, dear little fellow," says Mr. Maitland. "I accompanied him on several of his pony excursions, and the more I saw of him, the better I liked him."

Leech was entered at Charterhouse in 1824, Maitland a year or two afterwards, having grown into a strapping boy of eleven. Mr. Maitland's father was a Dean of St. Paul's, able, no doubt, from his position to procure a presentation—as he did from Lord Grey—for his son, who entered as a Gown boy, thus taking, and maintaining, a higher position in the school than Leech ever succeeded in reaching. Young Maitland had been a few days in the Charterhouse, when he was accosted by a small boy, who was obliged to tell his name before his early friend could recognise him. Boy-like, Maitland immediately took young Leech under his protection, and threatened dire consequences to anyone who bullied or ill-treated him. The protector's prowess, however, was not wanted, for Leech never made an enemy then or afterwards.

Amongst the scholars was one named Douglas, whose powers of sketching in caricature were very remarkable. Of this I convinced myself by a book of drawings in the possession of Mr. Maitland. Douglas's talent made him very attractive to Leech, and the boys became great friends.

"Leech copied several of his friend's drawings," says Mr. Maitland; but, as might have been expected, he soon abandoned copying and took to original work, a specimen of which I give below, as perhaps the earliest known drawing by Leech.[A]

If, before I had written the first portion of this book, I had known Mr. Maitland's story, I should have introduced it earlier; for this and other shortcomings and irregularities, I hope to be forgiven on the ground of my inexperience and ignorance of the laws of literary composition. With this apology I proceed to make more mistakes, but mistakes only in the *order* in which the *truth* should be told.

CHAPTER X.

LEECH AND HIS PREDECESSORS.

John Leech may be truly said to be *sui generis*; there has been nothing like him before his time, or since his bright and short career ended. It would be difficult to imagine a greater contrast than that existing between the works of Leech and those of his predecessors, at the head and front of whom must be placed Hogarth, who stands *longo intervallo* above any of his successors. In his terrible lashing of the vices and follies of his own time—vices and follies that are common to all time—Hogarth sometimes, though rarely, indulged in an exaggeration of character amounting to caricature. Leech dealt with the life about him in a totally different spirit; his was a lighter, a more genial, and a kinder hand. Unlike Hogarth, he made us laugh at the follies of our fellow-creatures, and would have nothing to do with their vices, though he has shown us in many examples how keen was his sympathy with the poor and the oppressed, and how intense was his hatred of the oppressor. The name of caricaturist is as inappropriate to Leech as it is to Hogarth, though instances may be found, as in Hogarth, of occasional indulgence in exaggeration. These examples are mostly to be found in the illustration of books which in themselves somewhat outrage the modesty of nature. Hogarth's pictures are often disfigured by a coarseness closely bordering on indecency; instances may, indeed, be found where the great artist has passed the border with revolting audacity. In the thousands of drawings by Leech, instead of the *double entendre*, we have some delightful trait of child-life; instead of the adulterous husband, we have paterfamilias living a healthy, happy life among his children, only amused at his schoolboy son's tricks played upon his sisters.

Consideration should, no doubt, be shown to Hogarth and his immediate successors in respect of the coarseness of the time in which they lived; certainly the works of Bunbury, Woodward, Rowlandson and Gillray require all the excuses that can be made for them. Compared to the two latter-named artists, the two former may be said to be harmless. In the hands of all four, however, caricature reigned triumphant.

Rowlandson had less excuse for the constant displays of vulgarity and ugliness that abound in his works, than the other designers, who were destitute of any sense of beauty. It was not so with Rowlandson. I have seen early drawings by him full of the charm of beauty in women: refined, and graceful. This power, which one would have thought was a part of the man's nature, vanished altogether as he advanced in life; swamped in the whirl of dissipation in which he lived, his originally better nature became utterly vulgarized by his surroundings. That Rowlandson had a certain very coarse humour, a facility in grouping masses of figures in large compositions, and a power of inventing faces and figures for which he had no authority in nature, cannot be denied; but there is always an intense vulgarity, in which the man seems to revel with as intense a pleasure.

Gillray altogether differed from Rowlandson, both in his subjects and in the way he treated them. In politics he was a savage partisan, lashing his opponents with merciless fury and cruel personality. Gillray was in art what Churchill was in literature. He had a grim humour all his own; witness his constant attacks upon Bonaparte, then, and always, the *bête noire* of this country. There are many examples in which the Corsican tyrant is made ridiculous, ferocious, or cowardly, according to the events of the time and the humour of the artist.

In a parody of Belshazzar's feast, Bonaparte, as Belshazzar, has caught sight of the writing on the wall; he looks with extended arms and an expression of cowardly horror at the warning. By his side sits the Empress, an outrage upon the fattest of fat women, ill-drawn and vulgar in the extreme. A man with a face hideous beyond the dreams of ugliness (caricature *in excelsis*) is devouring the Tower of London, which figures as a *plat* in the banquet; the rest of the guests round the monarch's table, vying with the dreadful gourmand in repulsiveness, are one and all caricatured out of nature. The meats provided for this singular entertainment consist of what may be called English fare, the *pièce de résistance* in front of Bonaparte, which he will presently demolish, being the Bank of England; and that indigestible dish is flanked by St. James's Palace. Then we have the head of Pitt, which is labelled "The Roast Beef of Old England," and served up appetizingly on a trencher, etc. Behind the Emperor stand his guards with huge uplifted sabres, from which blood is dripping, while behind the dropsical Empress stand her ladies-in-waiting, three female ghouls of wondrous hideousness, in dresses so *décolleté* as to shock persons less nice than Mrs. Grundy.

In another example the great Corsican is represented as "Teddy Doll, the great French Gingerbread Baker, drawing out a new Batch of Kings," while his man, Talleyrand, is making up the dough for others. Bonaparte is pictured in uniform, with boots and spurs, and a huge cocked-hat with an impossible feather, drawing out a batch of newly-made kings—Bavaria, Würtemburg, and Baden—from an enormous oven, labelled "New French Oven for Imperial Gingerbread." Beneath the oven-door is what is called "an ash-hole for broken gingerbread." Amongst the *débris* which has been swept into the ash-hole by a broom labelled "Corsican Besom of Destruction," Spain, a crowned death's head, is prominent; together with Austria, Holland, Switzerland, Venice, etc., "all in wild destruction blent." In the background Hanover is being destroyed by the Prussian Eagle, as Talleyrand is busy kneading up the dough to be presently passed from "the Political Kneading-Trough," to reappear in the shape of gingerbread kings of Poland, Turkey, and Hungary, after the manipulation of the King-maker and a visit to the French oven.

There is much grim humour in this piece, and humour as well as a deeper meaning in the parody of "Belshazzar's Feast"; but, turning from such work and the thoughts that arise from it to that of Leech is like turning from a slaughter-house to a flower-garden, from ugliness to beauty.

From the time of Gillray to that of Leech, there is little to be said of the caricaturists, with one splendid exception, "Immortal George." I do not agree with those who place Cruikshank above Leech. Cruikshank was essentially a caricaturist; Leech was not. Comparisons, as Mrs. Malaprop says, are "odorous," but we are sometimes forced into them; and, while admitting that there were certain paths—heights, perhaps—which Cruikshank ascended with honour, and on which Leech could not have found foothold, there was a highroad, bordered by beautiful things, on which he would have easily distanced his formidable rival.

In my young days the political drawings of "H. B.," the father of Richard Doyle, were much esteemed and in great request. They dealt solely with the political events of the hour, and, though feebly drawn and ineffective as works of art, the designer managed to produce unmistakable likenesses of Sir Robert Peel, the Duke of Wellington, *et hoc genus*, with remarkable certainty, and always without a trace of caricature.

CHAPTER XI.

KENNY MEADOWS.

The reader has only to look at the early numbers of *Punch* to see how inferior were the drawings compared to Leech's work, or to that of the excellent artists now at work on *Punch*. Kenny Meadows was perhaps the best; indeed, he was a fellow of excellent fancy, quaintly humorous at times—seen, I think, at his best in his Shakespeare illustrations; which, in spite of some extravagance, are full of character, and, as in the "Midsummer Night's Dream," almost poetical in their realization of the scenes of that immortal play. But Kenny was a sad Bohemian, a jovial soul, loving company and the refreshments that attend it, in which he indulged in happy forgetfulness till "all but he departed."

In illustration of Kenny's habits, I introduce a little story told to me by himself. Long years ago Mr. Carter Hall edited a book of British ballads, and engaged a number of artists to illustrate them; Kenny Meadows amongst the rest. I also had the honour of supplying a contribution. When the drawings were finished, we were invited one evening to the Rosery—as Mr. Hall called his Brompton cottage—to submit our work for his criticism, and approval or condemnation, as the case might be. Our refreshment was coffee and biscuits, a repast very unsatisfactory to all of us, more or less—to Meadows especially. Kenny bore his disappointment very well till we left the Rosery—this we did at the earliest moment consistent with good manners—when he said, after criticising our entertainment in strong language:

"There is a house close by where we can get supper. What do you fellows say?"

We all said "that was the place for us."

Under Meadows' guidance, we found an inn and an excellent supper, and about midnight, when the fun was getting fast and furious, I left; Meadows remaining with two or three other choice spirits—how long I only knew when I met him a few days afterwards. The time of his return home may be guessed by what follows. Day was breaking as Meadows stealthily entered his bedroom, almost praying that Mrs. Meadows might be asleep; but that lady awoke, and, catching sight of her husband, said:

"You are very late, Meadows."

"Oh no," said Meadows, "I am not; it's quite early."

("So it was, you know," said the Bohemian to me, as he told me of his reception.)

"Early!" exclaimed the wife. "Why, what o'clock is it?"

"Oh, about one, or a little after," said Kenny.

Unluckily, at that moment the peculiar but unmistakable cry of the milkman was heard—"and that pretty well settled the time, you know, Frith."

CHAPTER XII.

"COMIC HISTORY OF ROME."

The extreme difficulty—in some instances the impossibility—of procuring copies of some of the books illustrated by Leech makes exact chronological sequence impossible in any attempt to describe the career of the artist. I hope to be pardoned, therefore, for the irregularity of my dates.

In 1852 a "Comic History of Rome" appeared, written by Gilbert à Beckett, with "ten coloured etchings and numerous woodcuts by Leech." Rome fares pretty much the same as England at the hands of both writer and illustrator. In Mr. À Beckett's part of the work the history of Rome becomes a very comic history indeed, and Leech, of course, enters into the spirit of the fun with all his exuberance of fancy and irresistible humour. Visitors to the National Gallery, should they be curious to see the difference of treatment of the same subject by different minds, can be gratified by comparing Rubens' "Rape of the Sabines" with Leech's rendering of that famous historical event.

In one particular the illustration of the scene is identical in both pictures. Rubens dresses the ladies in the costume peculiar to his own time; Leech in the time of Queen Victoria. In the great Fleming's work the principal victim of the Roman youth is the wife of the painter, in the dress of Rubens' day; in Leech's drawing, strange to say, we have an excellent likeness of Mrs. Leech, as she sits complacently on the shoulders of a Roman youth. Rubens, however, pays more attention to truth in the habiliments of his ravishers, for if they, in all probability, did not much resemble Roman soldiers in their habits as they lived, they present a tolerable resemblance to the ancient Roman as we know him. Whereas Leech—while preserving something like the form of the upper part of the Roman costume—cannot be said to be correct when he puts Hessian boots upon one man, hunting-tops upon another, and consigns the nether portion of a third to the military trousers, boots and spurs of the modern Life-Guardsman. Nobody, I think, will believe that umbrellas were known to the Romans, as Leech would have us to understand, by putting one as a weapon into the hands of the stout, very modern woman belabouring the Roman who is carrying off her daughter.

In explanation of the following cut, I may remind readers of Roman history that Romulus sent cards of invitation to attend certain games to the Latins and Sabines, with their wives and daughters.

"The weather being propitious," says Mr. À Beckett, "all the Sabine beauty and fashion were attracted to the place, and the games, consisting of horse-racing, gave to the scene all the animation of Ascot on a Cup-day. Suddenly, at a preconcerted signal, there was a general elopement of the Roman youth with the Sabine ladies, who were in the most ungallant manner abandoned to their fate by the Sabine gentlemen. It is true the latter were taken by surprise, but they certainly made the best of their way home before they thought of avenging the wrong and insult that had been committed. Had they been all married ladies who were carried off, the cynic might have suggested that the Sabine husbands would not have objected to a cheap mode of divorce; but—to make use of an Irishism—there was only one single woman who happened to be a wife in the whole of that goodly company."

ELOPEMENT OF ROMAN YOUTH WITH SABINE LADIES.

An Etruscan ruler named Porsenna had a difficulty with Rome. He speedily besieged that city, frightening the people in the suburbs "out of their wits and into the city, where he never enjoyed a moment's peace till peace was concluded." Presently a treaty of peace was negotiated, greatly to the advantage of Porsenna; for not only was Rome compelled to restore the territory taken from the Veii, but the victor also "claimed hostages, among whom were sundry young ladies of the principal Roman families. One of these was named Clælia, who, with other maidens, having resolved on a bold plunge for their liberty, jumped into the Tiber's bed, and swam like a party of ducks to the other side of the river."

This delightful drawing reminds one of many a seaside sketch in "Pictures of

Life and Character," leaving us wondering how a few pencil-lines can call up such visions of beauty.

Everyone knows of the tradition of Rome's being saved from the Gauls by the cackling of geese, and my readers are here presented with Leech's historical picture of the event.

ROME SAVED FROM THE GAULS BY GEESE.

"The Gauls," says Mr. À Beckett, "crept up, one by one, to the top of the rock, which was the summit of their wishes. Just as they had effected their object, a wakeful goose commenced a vehement cackle, and the solo of one old bird was soon followed by a chorus from a score of others. Marcus Manlius, who resided near the poultry, was so alarmed at the sound that he instantly jumped out of his skin—for in those days a sheep-skin was the usual bedding—and ran to the spot, where he caught hold of the first Gaul he came to, and, giving him a smart push, the whole pack behind fell like so many cards to the bottom."

CHAPTER XIII.

PERSONAL ANECDOTES.

The late Frederick Tayler, whose water-colour drawings are familiar to all lovers of art, was a guest for some days at the mansion of the Duke of Athole —an elderly gentleman thirty years ago, but how nearly connected with the present Duke I am unable to say. According to Tayler, the old Duke was a very eccentric person; one of his whims being an insistence upon all the male guests at his castle wearing the Scottish national dress. On my friend's pleading that he could not wear a costume that he didn't possess, he was supplied with the kilt and the rest of it, from a store kept for unprovided visitors—"and," said Tayler, "I was immediately compelled to ride about eighteen miles in a condition of discomfort that may be imagined." Another little peculiarity was scarcely less distressing, for dinner was never served till near midnight. Hungry guests were kept waiting till, folding-doors being thrown open, the major-domo appeared, holding a wand, and in solemn tones announced "His Grace!"

In 1850 this remarkable Duke "took it into his head" to close his beautiful Glen Tilt to tourists. I was fortunate enough to have passed through it before this decree was issued; but multitudes—noisy multitudes, as they proved themselves—not having had my advantage, became clamorous for their right, as they believed, of unobstructed passage through the lovely glen. Many letters from indignant tourists appeared in the press, which almost universally condemned the Duke's action, *Punch's* baton being brought into play in the tourists' cause; and to this weapon was added Leech's pencil, which, in a vigorous drawing, portrayed the old Duke as a dog in the manger, with a snarl on his face that portended a bite if his position was assailed. The drawing was entitled "A Scotch Dog in the Manger," and was immediately followed by another blow, happily paraphrasing Scott's lines in the "Lady of the Lake," and supposed to apply to "a scene from the burlesque recently performed at Glen Tilt":

"These are Clan Athole's warriors true,
  And, Saxons, I'm the regular Doo."

How far these drawings were the means of causing the Duke to reverse his decision I know not; but it was reversed, and that he took Leech's somewhat severe treatment good-humouredly is shown by his treatment of the artist, whom he met near the glen soon after the drawings appeared. Leech was alone, sketch-book in hand, no doubt noting, by pencil and observation, for future use, some of the beauties around him, when a horseman approached, attended by a groom. Leech was probably on forbidden ground, for the rider, who was the Duke of Athole, immediately asked his name and "what he was doing there." Under ordinary circumstances Leech would have said, "What is *your* name?" for the matter of that, "and what do you want to do with mine if I give it to you?"; but whether the manner of his questioner impressed him, or conscious guilt shook him, I cannot say. It is certain, however, that he replied he was an artist, and that his name was Leech.

"Not John Leech?" said the Duke.

"Yes, John," was the reply.

And Leech now, feeling sure that he was in the presence of the Duke, and that he was about to hear some strong language about his daring to caricature so august a personage for merely asserting his rights, proceeded to explain that he would not intrude further, but return at once to his inn, where he intended to pass the night.

The Duke turned to his groom, and told him to dismount, and called to Leech to take the servant's place.

Leech obeyed, when the Duke said, "No, sir; no inn for you to-night: you must dine and sleep at my house. I am the Duke of Athole." Further hesitation on Leech's part was met by a warmer and more pressing invitation.

Leech yielded, and the two rode off together. The road to the castle lay through some rather perilous country, culminating in a narrow and broken path, with cliff on one side and a precipice on the other. The artist hesitated; the Duke called upon him to come on. "Has he brought me here to revenge himself by breaking my neck?" thought Leech. He timidly advanced, and reached the Duke, who had stopped for him at a point where the path was most dangerous.

"Are you, sir, the man who has maligned me in *Punch?*" fiercely demanded the Duke.

The fearful position in which Leech found himself, terrible to anyone, but to a nervous man especially frightful, extorted from him an apologetic confession, excusable under the circumstances.

"Your Grace," said he, "we—we—that is, nearly everyone—has done something that he—he—regrets having done. I am very sorry I have—— I regret very much that anything I have done should have given you any annoyance."

The Duke's affected fierceness was exchanged for the jovial manner said to

59

be peculiar to him, and the pair rode off pleasantly together.

The castle was reached, and Leech was shown to a dressing-room, where he made himself as presentable as he could under the circumstances, in anticipation of the usual announcement that dinner was served. I can imagine my friend's feelings as he waited in hungry expectation. "As he could not manage to break my neck," thought Leech, as hour after hour passed without a summons to dinner, "he means to starve me."

At last, thinking that perhaps his room was too far off for the sound of the gong to reach him, he rang the bell. A servant appeared.

"I am afraid," said Leech, "that I did not hear the dinner-bell; is dinner ready?"

"Not yet, sir; you will be informed when it is."

Another hour passed. Leech became desperate; starvation seemed to stare him in the face. Again he rang the bell; again the servant answered it, and the reply was again, "Not yet."

The clock had struck ten before the welcome sound of the gong reached the famished man. If Mr. Frederick Tayler is to be believed, the Leech dinner with the Duke was an *early* one. No explanation was ever given to Tayler of these abnormal dinner-hours, but Leech was told that "his Grace" always took a nap after his rides, and his guests were fed when he awoke.

Leech was fond of telling of this adventure with the Duke, whose likeness can be seen in more than one of Landseer's pictures.

CHAPTER XIV.

PERSONAL ANECDOTES (*continued*).

At the time when the troop of artists and literary men were stumping the country with their theatrical performances, Leech lived in Alfred Place, which he soon left for a charming little house in Notting Hill Terrace.

Dickens wrote an amusing account of one of the amateur excursions, which the immortal Mrs. Gamp is supposed to join, and about which she discourses to her friend Mrs. Harris, not forgetting her opinion of the artists, Cruikshank and Leech:

"If you'll believe me, Mrs. Harris, I turns my head, and sees the very man" (George Cruikshank) "a-making pictures of me on his thumb-nail at the window; while another of 'em" (John Leech), "a tall, slim, melancolly gent, with dark hair and a bage voice, looks over his shoulder, and with his head o' one side, as if he understood the subject, and coolly he says:

"'I've drawed her several times in *Punch*,' he says, too. The owdacious wretch!

"'Which I never touches, Mr. Wilson,' I says out loud—I couldn't have helped it, Mrs. Harris, if you'd took my life for it—'which I never touches, Mr. Wilson, on account of the lemon!'"

From the nature of Leech's work, he was never able to take a holiday in the true sense of the word. To say nothing of the numberless works which he had engaged himself to illustrate, the inevitable *Punch* must appear every week, and almost equally inevitable was the appearance of one or two of Leech's drawings in it. Proof is abundant of the rapidity with which those inimitable works were executed; but it must be borne in mind that they were the outcome of a sensitive organization—a power of seeing and seizing the humorous and the beautiful in the everyday incidents of life; in short, of a mind always on the watch for subjects for illustration.

When one thinks of the constant wear and tear of such a life, it is scarcely a matter for wonder that it was so lamentably short.

The localities of Leech's so-called holidays can easily be recognised by his drawings, or rather by their backgrounds, which showed, in admirable truthfulness, whether the artist was at Scarborough or Broadstairs, at Folkestone, Dover, Lowestoft, or Ramsgate, or, by their unfamiliarity to us, at some less frequented place.

It was in 1848, and while Mr. and Mrs. Leech were staying with the Dickens family at Brighton, that a very unpleasant incident of the visit took place: no less than the sudden insanity of the landlord of the house in which the party lodged, resulting in as sudden an exeunt of the lodgers. But before the people still in their senses could take themselves off, there was a duty to be done. A doctor must be fetched; and no sooner did he appear than the madman attacked him, and would very soon have made a vacancy in the list of M.D.'s if Dickens and Leech had not rushed to the rescue. In a letter to Forster, Dickens gives a humorous description of Mrs. Leech and Mrs. Dickens doing their best—in their fear for their husbands' safety—to assist the maniac in his murderous endeavours by pulling their husbands back just as the doctor had fainted from fear. More assistance, however, arrived, and the mad landlord was soon rendered harmless.

I vividly recollect the alarm that the news of an accident to Leech—in which it was rumoured that he had been seriously, even dangerously, injured— caused to everyone, and acutely to his friends. A huge wave was said to have struck him while bathing—killing him on the spot, according to some reports; fracturing his skull, or producing concussion of the brain, from which recovery was hopeless, according to others. These alarming accounts came to us from the Isle of Wight, where Leech was staying with Dickens in the autumn of 1849. The fact was, that one of the tremendous waves that, under certain atmospheric conditions, roll in upon the shore at Bonchurch, struck Leech on the forehead, and rendered him senseless.

"He was put to bed," said Dickens, "with twenty of his namesakes upon his temples."

The day following, congestion of the brain became unmistakable, accompanied by great pain; ice was applied to the head, and bleeding again was thought necessary, this time in the arm. For some days Leech was in great danger, Dickens sitting up with him all night on more than one alarming occasion. He says, in a letter to Forster:

"My plans are all unsettled by Leech's illness, as of course I do not like to leave this place so long as I can be of any service to him and his good little wife. Ever since I wrote to you he has been seriously worse, and again very heavily bled. The night before last he was in such an alarming state of restlessness, which nothing could relieve, that I proposed to Mrs. Leech to try magnetism. Accordingly, in the middle of the night, I fell to, and, after a very fatiguing bout of it, put him to sleep for an hour and thirty-five minutes. A change came on in his sleep, and he is decidedly better. I talked to the astounded Mrs. Leech across him, when he was asleep, as if he had been a truss of hay."

Whether from Dickens' magnetic efforts or the efforts of Nature, Leech gradually, but very slowly, recovered. On being questioned about his accident, Leech is reported to have said that he remembered an enormous angry, white-topped wave coming at him, and, in what seemed to him the next moment, he found himself in bed in great pain—the interval having been some days.

In corroboration of this, I may mention an accident that happened to Mr. Elmore (brother of the R.A. and great friend of Leech), who was terribly injured by a blow on the head in a railway accident on the Marseilles line.

"I was reading a novel," said Mr. Elmore to me, "and the next instant, as it seemed, I found myself suffering great pain in a strange bed, with strange surroundings, in what I afterwards found was a French cottage."

The sufferer also found that more than three weeks had elapsed between the blow and the recovery of consciousness from it. Where, in my blind ignorance I venture to ask, was the ever-living soul all this time?

One of the amusements of the visitors at Folkestone consists in watching the arrival of the French packet; and I have noticed that the more stormy the day, the greater is the crowd that forms itself into an avenue, through which the voyagers must pass in landing. This amusement, I think, is not very creditable to us, because it is derived from an enjoyment arising from the sufferings of our fellow-creatures. The rosy passenger, who is evidently "a good sailor," attracts no attention—we rather resent his condition as inappropriate to the occasion; but the man from whose face every vestige of colour has flown, whose legs can scarcely support him as he walks up the gangway, is an object of great delight to us. We are generally—not always—silent in our enjoyment, scarcely ever receiving a poor sea-sick creature as Leech was once welcomed at Boulogne.

In 1854, Leech and his wife went to Boulogne to stay with Dickens. The day was stormy, and when the artist stepped ashore, he was received with cheers by a crowd of people, mostly English, who loudly congratulated him as looking more intensely miserable than any of the wretched passengers who had preceded him. Leech told Dickens that he had realized at last what an actor's feelings must be when a round of applause greets his efforts.

"I felt," he said, "that I had made a great hit."

My intimacy with Leech led to the usual exchange of hospitalities. I recall with pleasure the occasions on which I had the great delight of welcoming him at my house in London or at the seaside. He never varied from the simple, modest demeanour of the perfect gentleman, was never noisy or argumentative, and always considerate of the feelings of others; prodigal in his praise of his brother artists; never, if he could avoid it, speaking of himself or his works, but if, in course of conversation, allusion had been made to some cut more than commonly attractive, he would meet it with: "Glad you like it, my dear fellow; don't see anything particularly funny in it myself;" or, "Ah! I wish you could have seen it on the wood; they seem to me to have cut all the prettiness out of the girl's face."

The first time I dined with Leech was at his house in Notting Hill Terrace, on the occasion of some Highland sports that took place in Lord Holland's park hard by, out of which Leech made some capital sketches, that afterwards appeared in *Punch*. Leech's dinners, without being too lavish or extravagant, were always unexceptionable as to food, and notably so as to wine; of the latter, being no judge himself, he took care it should be supplied by "one who knew," and who was also reliable. One of the guests at this particular dinner was the Rev. Mr. White, whose acquaintance our host had made at the Isle of Wight. I mention this gentleman because he was not only a very jovial clergyman, but a great friend of Leech and Dickens, and the author of some plays which had more or less success—one of them, with the title of "The King of the Commons," was played under Phelps' management, and had a considerable run.

"White," Leech whispered to me, "is a great judge of port. I hope to goodness he will like some I have got on purpose for him—and for you, my boy; only you know nothing about it, do you?"

"Not a bit," said I.

When the port appeared we watched the clergyman, and, judging by his expression, the port was successful; but Leech was not satisfied till in reply to his inquiry as to its qualities the clergyman, smacking his lips, said:

"Sir, the Church approves."

At one of the delightful dinners at Leech's double-windowed house—double-windowed to keep out noise, which distressed him all his life—on the Terrace, Kensington, I first met Shirley Brooks, thus commencing a life-long friendship with one of the most charming companions, one of the wittiest men and the best story-tellers that ever made "the hours go by on rosy wing." One of the strongest men on the *Punch* staff—afterwards editor—Brooks and Leech became somewhat intimate, but whether the intimacy ever became merged into close friendship, I doubt. I frequently dined at Brooks's, but never met Leech there—indeed, from what I have heard, I am pretty sure that, with the exception of his old fellow-student, Percival Leigh, who was one of his nearest and dearest friends, Leech's feeling towards his brother members of the *Punch* staff never reached friendship in the true meaning of the word. Albert Smith, of whose entertainments Leech said one of the severest things I or anyone ever heard him say—"After all, Frith, it is only bad John Parry"—was a loud, and, to me, a rather vulgar person—too antagonistic to the gentle Leech for the growth of friendship. At the *Punch* meetings, however, I have it from one who was occasionally present, that Albert Smith always addressed Leech as "Jack," being the only one of the company who used the familiarity. This provoked Douglas Jerrold, who had often winced under the infliction, to ask Leech one day, "How long is it necessary for a man to know you before he can call you 'Jack'?"

After this remark "Jack" was less frequently heard. My authority for the above is the late Mr. George Hodder, an author who I fear has left no "footprints in the sands of time." It was said of him that, on being introduced to a very distinguished artist, he remarked—perhaps feeling the necessity of making a complimentary speech—"Art is a grand thing, sir." This unfortunate gentleman died from injuries received by the upsetting of a coach in Richmond Park.

It is not at all uncommon for middle-class entertainers—though they may possess a fair staff of servants—to seek outside assistance when they gather an unusual number of guests round their hospitable boards. On one occasion —and very likely oftener—Leech sought such supplementary aid, and found it in the form of his parish clerk, a solemn person who was not too proud to add to his stipend by "going out to wait." As is usual with his class, the clerk-waiter arrived in good time to help in furnishing forth the dinner-table, having an eye to the placing of the flowers, plate, etc. The guests, amounting to ten or twelve, were announced in due course, all old acquaintances, and all expecting their dinners with the punctuality for which their host was noted. Hungry men, though they may be good talkers under happier circumstances, are seldom brilliant; on this occasion, though Dickens and Jerrold may have been amongst the guests, the conversation languished at last into silence. Half an hour passed. What could have happened? Suddenly one of the guests—was it Dickens or Jerrold?—sprang from his chair, and going to Leech, with extended hand, said:

"Well, it's getting late; I'm afraid I must go. Thank you, dear boy, for a delightful evening; the dinner was capital, the turtle first rate—never tasted finer salmon; and as to the champagne——"

The puzzled looks of Leech and his guests ended in a roar of laughter, in the midst of which a black and solemn figure appeared, and in the tones in which he would have given the responses at church, said:

"Dinner is served."

The assembled guests received the welcome announcement with a chorus of

"Amen!"

CHAPTER XV.

SPORTING NOVELS.

Amongst the many books illustrated by Leech are some sporting novels, written, I think, by a Mr. Surtees. "Ask Mamma," "Handley Cross," "Plain or Ringlets," "Mr. Romford's Hounds," etc., owe their origin to this prolific gentleman. As these works are ornamented by coloured steel engravings and innumerable woodcuts by Leech, it has been my duty to look into them; read them, I cannot. I hope if the author is still living he will attribute my want of appreciation to a want of sympathy with his heroes and heroines, though I admit, in the portions I have read, that he shows considerable humour as well as power in expressing it. This, from one who knows his own ignorance of the subject in question, should be gratifying to Mr. Surtees.

Though to my mind Leech is quite at his best in "Pictures of Life and Character," there are examples of his powers in all these books which quite justify my selection of some of them for the gratification of my readers. "Mr. Romford's Hounds" is "embellished" with twenty-five large steel plates, in one of which a certain Mr. Facey, who has a charming Miss Lucy for his hunting companion, is checked by an obstacle which causes him to exclaim to Lucy, "Dash it! this is a rum customer," "as he stood in his stirrups, looking at what was on the far side."

"Oh, throw your heart over it," said Lucy, "and then follow it as quickly as you can."

"Heart!" muttered Facey. "I shall never find it again if I do. It would be like looking for a needle in a bundle of hay."

"Let *me* try, then," said Lucy.

It would be difficult indeed to surpass the beauty of the girl's figure in this drawing, exquisitely drawn, true in character and action as it is. Mr. Facey's expression, too, exactly conveys the idea that the longer he looks at the awkward place the less he likes it. The horses—notably the action of the one ridden by the young lady—are in every way admirable. The background, with a few slight touches, gives us a stretch of country—a withered tree, a flock of birds, and the cloudy sky, with no doubt the southerly wind that "proclaims the hunting morning."

"Mr. Romford's Hounds" gives us another sportsman, who rejoices in the name of Muffington. This gentleman is possessed for the moment of a horse called, or, rather, miscalled, Placid Joe, whose former name, Pull Devil, seems better-suited to his propensities, as shown in the drawing, in which Placid Joe has taken the bit between his teeth, to the discomfiture of Mr. Muffington. From the following telegram it would seem that Placid Joe had been borrowed for the day's hunting. Thus it ran:

"Mr. Martin Muffington, at the White Swan, Showoffborough, to Mr. Green, Brown Street, Bagnigge Wells Road, London.

"That brute Placid Joe has no more mouth than a bull. He's carried me right into the midst of the hounds, and nearly annihilated the huntsman. I will send him back by the 9.30 a.m. train to-morrow, and won't pay you a halfpenny for his hire."

The character of Mr. Muffington, together with his action as he tugs in vain at Placid Joe, are admirable; but the horse, good as it is in action, appears to me less well proportioned than Leech's horses almost invariably are, the head and neck being too small. But what could surpass the huntsman and his steed just recovering from the "cannoning" received from Placid Joe? The scattered hounds, the riders behind, and the landscape leave nothing to be desired.

"Plain or Ringlets" contains twelve coloured plates and no less than forty-three woodcuts. Judging from a slight acquaintance with the letterpress and a careful study of the illustrations in this book, I find that the author deals less exclusively with the feats of the hunter than in "Mr. Romford's Hounds"; shooting, racing, etc., are allowed to figure prominently, and the pursuit of "lovely woman"—in which there seem to be as many false scents and heavy falls as beset the chasing of the fox—plays an important part in "Plain or Ringlets." Unlike the policeman's, I have often thought that the riding-master's life must "be a happy one." I am borne out in this, I think, by the illustration, in which Leech is delightfully at home. Says our author:

"Smiling, cantering bevies of beauties, with their shining hair in gold or silver beaded nets, and party-coloured feathers in their jaunty little hats, alone imparted energy to the scene as they tit-tupped along with quickly following tramp, led by the most magnificent and affable of riding-masters, who thus advertise their studs, just as Howes and Cushing advertise their grand United States Circus. Bless us, what a pace some of them go!"

What life and motion there are in this group! How is it, by what occult influence do we find those two lovely creatures right and left of the riding-master, instead of one place of honour being reserved for the stout middle-aged lady, who, strange to say, seems quite contented with her position? I don't believe those two girls want any teaching, for do they not sit their horses with perfect grace, as safely at home in their saddles as they would be in one of the lounges in their drawing-rooms, which either of them would fill so charmingly? Look what pretty creatures the magician Leech can call up for us by a few scratches of his pencil, in the rear of this cantering procession!

The Duke of Tergiversation (Phœbus, what a name!), says the author of "Plain or Ringlets," found on inheriting his estate that "the life had been eaten out of it" before the death of his father put him in possession of his ancestral property. The Duke, however, seems to have made the acquaintance of a banker, named Goldspink, who yielded to his persuasions and promises to the extent of allowing his aristocratic customer to overdraw his account to such a formidable amount as seriously to imperil the stability of the bank. Mr. Goldspink then seeks an interview with his Grace, which the Duke, after endeavouring by all sorts of shifts to avoid, was at length compelled to grant.

"Ah, my dear Mr. Goldspink!" exclaimed the Duke, advancing with outstretched hands and all the cheerful cordiality imaginable as our "crab-actioned" friend followed the smoothly-gliding butler, Mr. Garnett, into the presence. "Ah, my dear Goldspink, this is indeed most kind and considerate! First neighbour that has come to greet us. How, may I ask, is your worthy wife and your excellent son?" taking both the banker's hands and shaking them severely.

The banker makes a mental calculation of the Duke's liabilities, with a clear understanding that "his Grace is on the gammon-and-spinach tack," and then says:

"Thank your Grace—his Grace—my Grace—that is to say—they are both pretty well. Hope the Duchess and Lord Marchhare——"

"The Duchess and Marchhare are both at this moment enjoying a quiet cup of tea in her pretty little boudoir, where, I am sure, they will be most happy to see Mr. Goldspink," said the Duke, motioning him to the gilt-moulded white door opposite.

This cut seems to me to show Leech's power of marking the difference of character in the persons represented in a degree noticeable by the most ordinary observer. The Duke is an aristocrat from top to toe; the insincerity of his welcome even is apparent; while the squat and "crab-like" figure of the banker is no less true to nature; his delight at shaking hands with a Duke making him forget for the moment the serious issues dependent upon the interview.

At the eleventh hour I find myself forbidden to show my readers any of the admirable drawings which illustrate this book.

CHAPTER XVI.

THE "BON GAULTIER BALLADS."

I will here leave the sporting novels for a time and introduce my reader to the "Bon Gaultier Ballads," and if he make his first acquaintance with that work through this introduction, I respectfully advise him to improve it by a more intimate knowledge, for he will not only find excellent reading, but illustrations by Richard Doyle and others, scarcely inferior to those by Leech.

It will be remembered that at the time of the Papal aggression Lord John Russell, according to Leech, chalked "No Popery" on Cardinal Wiseman's door and then ran away. In the "Bon Gaultier Ballads" we find his lordship face to face with Cardinal Wiseman, disguised as a friar, in Sherwood Forest, where Little John is supposed to reign in place of Robin Hood, deceased. The ballad is entitled "Little John and the Red Friar," and begins:

"The deer may leap within the glade,
      The fawns may follow free—
   For Robin is dead, and his bones are laid
      Beneath the greenwood tree.

*   *   *   *   *

"Now, Little John was an outlaw proud,
      A prouder ye never saw;
   Through Nottingham and Leicestershires
      He thought his word was law,
   And he strutted through the greenwood wide
      Like a pestilent jackdaw.

*   *   *   *   *

"Now, word had come to Little John,
      As he lay upon the grass,
That a friar red was in merry Sherwood
      Without his leave to pass."

Little John inquires from his little foot-page what manner of man is this burly friar who intrudes into his domain.

"'My master good,' the little page said,
      'His name I wot not well;
   But he wears on his head a hat so red,
      With a monstrous scallop-shell.

"'He says he is Prior of Copmanhurst,
      And Bishop of London town,
   And he comes with a rope from our Father the Pope
      To put the outlaws down.'"

Little John searches the forest for his scarlet enemy—

"O'er holt and hill, through brake and breere,
      He took his way alone.

*   *   *   *   *

"Then Little John, he strutted on,
      Till he came to an open bound,
   And he was aware of a Red Friar
      Was sitting upon the ground.

"His shoulders they were broad and strong,
      And large was he of limb;

Few yeomen in the north countrie
    Would care to mell with him.

*   *   *   *   *

"'What dost thou here, thou strong friar,
    In Sherwood's merry round,
Without the leave of Little John
    To range with hawk and hound?'

"'Small thought have I,' quoth the Red Friar,
    'Of any leave, I trow;
But Little John is an outlawed thief,
    And so, I ween, art thou!

"'Know I am, I am Prior ofCopmanhurst,
    And Bishop of London town,
And I bring a rope from our Father thePope
    To put the outlaws down.'

"Then out spoke Little John in wrath,
    'I tell thee, burly frere,
The Pope may do as he likes at home,
    But he sends no Bishops here!'"

"'Up and away, Red Friar,' he said,
    'Up and away right speedilie;
And were it not for that cowl of thine,
    Avenged on thy body I would be!'

In silence and in grief found Gilkison relief,
   Nor did Neish the spell-word 'beef'
                           Dare to breathe."

Then Edith, the bride, made her appearance upon the ramparts.

"And she said unto her lord, as he leaned upon his sword,
   'One short and little word may I speak?
I cannot bear to view those eyes so ghastly blue,
   Or mark the sallow hue
                           Of thy cheek.

"'I know the rage and wrath that my furious brother hath
   Is less against us both than at me.
Then, dearest, let me go, to find among the foe
   An arrow from the bow,
                           Like Broomlee!'"

To this noble offer of self-sacrifice Sir Launcelot will not listen for a moment.
He replies:

"'All our chances are not lost, as your brother and his host
   Shall discover to their cost rather hard!
Ho, Provan! take this key; hoist up the malvoisie,
   And heap it, d'ye see,
                           In the yard.

"'Of usquebaugh and rum you will find, I reckon, some,
   Beside the beer and mum, extra stout;
Go straightway to your task, and roll me all the casks,
   And also range the flasks
                           Just without.

"'If I know the Gorbaliers, they are sure to dip their ears
   In the very inmost tiers of the drink.
Let them win the outer court, and hold it for their sport,
   Since their time is rather short,
                           I should think!'

"With a loud triumphant yell, as the heavy drawbridge fell,
   Rushed the Gorbaliers pell-mell, wild as Druids;
Mad with thirst for human gore, how they threatened and they swore,
   Till they stumbled on the floor
                           O'er the fluids.

"Down their weapons then they threw, and each savage soldier drew
   From his belt an iron screw in his fist;

George of Gorbals found it vain their excitement to restrain,
　　And, indeed, was rather fain

　　　　　　　　To assist.

"With a beaker in his hand, in the midst he took his stand,
　　And silence did command all below;
　'Ho, Launcelot the bold! ere thy lips are icy cold,
　　In the centre of thy hold

　　　　　　　　Pledge me now!'

*　　*　　*　　*　　*

"Dumb as death stood Launcelot, as though he heard him not;
　　But his bosom Provan smote and he swore,
And Sir Roderick Dalgleish remarked aside to Neish,
　　'Never, sure, did thirsty fish

　　　　　　　　Swallow more!

"'Thirty casks are nearly done, yet the revel's scarce begun;
　　It were knightly sport and fun to strike in!'
　'Nay, tarry till they come,' quoth Neish, 'unto the rum—
　　They are working at the mum

　　　　　　　　And the gin!'

"Then straight there did appear to each gallant Gorbalier
　　Twenty castles dancing near, all around;
The solid earth did shake, and the stones beneath them quake,
　　And sinuous as a snake

　　　　　　　　Moved the ground.

"Why and wherefore had they come seemed intricate unto some,
　　But all agreed the rum was divine;
And they looked with bitter scorn on their leader highly born,
　　Who preferred to fill his horn

　　　　　　　　Up with wine."

Like the fateful moment at Waterloo, the time had now come to strike, and Sir
Launcelot and his friends took full advantage of it.

"'Now make the trumpets blast, and comrades follow fast,
　　Smite them down unto the last,'

　　　　　　　　Cried the knight.

*　　*　　*　　*　　*

"Saint Mungo be my guide! it was goodly in that tide
　　To see the Bogle ride in his haste;

78

He accompanied each blow with a cry of 'ah!' or 'oh!'
    As he always cleft the foe
                To the waist.

"'George of Gorbals, craven lord! thou didst threat me with the cord;
    Come forth and brave my sword, if you dare!'
But he met with no reply, and never could descry
    The glitter of his eye
                Anywhere."

The Gorbaliers were destroyed to a man, and in obedience to an order from Sir Launcelot the casks and empty flasks were removed by the "cellar master," but not without a shock—

"For he swore he heard a shriek
                Through the door.

"When the merry Christmas came, and the Yule-log lent its flame
    To the face of squire and dame in the hall,
The cellarer went down to tap October brown,
    Which was rather of renown
                'Mongst them all.

"He placed the spigot low, and gave the cask a blow,
    But his liquor would not flow through the pin;
'Sure, 'tis sweet as honeysuckles!' so he rapped it with his knuckles,
    But a sound as if of buckles
                Clashed within.

"'Bring a hatchet, varlets, here!' and they cleft the cask of beer—
    What a spectacle of fear met their sight!
There George of Gorbals lay, skull and bones all blanched and gray,
    In the arms he bore the day
                Of the fight!"

GEORGE OF GORBALS.

From Leech's contributions to the "Bon Gaultier Ballads" my third selection consists of an illustration of "The Lay of the Lover's Friend." The "Lay" is a capital skit on the propensity of certain lovers to inflict the sorrows caused by the loss of their hearts upon friends to whom the loss is a matter of indifference. Says the friend:

THE LOVER'S FRIEND AND THE LOVER.

"'I would all womankind were dead,

Or banished o'er the sea;
For they have been a bitter plague
   These last six weeks to me.
It is not that I am touched myself,
    For that I do not fear;
 No female face has shown me grace
    For many a bygone year.
      But 'tis the most infernal bore,
        Of all the bores I know,
      To have a friend who's lost his heart
        A short time ago.

"'Whene'er we steam it to Blackwall,
   Or down to Greenwich run,
To quaff the pleasant cider-cup,
   Or feed on fish and fun;
Or climb the slopes of Richmond Hill
   To catch a breath of air—
Then, for my sins, he straight begins
   To rave about his fair.
      Oh, 'tis the most tremendous bore,
        Of all the bores I know,
      To have a friend who's lost his heart
        A short time ago.'"

Judging from the angry face of "the lover's friend" as he stretches out his hand towards the claret, it will require even more than the consolation to be derived from the finest brand to enable him to endure his friend's moaning with common patience. One studies with wonder and admiration the few touches with which the story is told in this little drawing. See the handsome frowning face of "the lover's friend," so perfectly in contrast with that of the absorbed lover, whose voice can almost be heard expatiating on the beauty of the lost one, and the hardness of her heart!

CHAPTER XVII.

Sporting Novels (*continued*).

"Handley Cross" is another of the sporting novels so admirably illustrated by Leech. The hero of this book is a certain Mr. Jorrocks, a retired "great city grocer of the old school." A fortune gained in the grocery business enabled Mr. Jorrocks to retire into country life, where the sports of the field awaited him. He became a mighty hunter, the possessor of the finest horses and "the best pack of 'ounds in all the world," who would make the foxes cry "Capevi!" He is M.F.H., and so great an authority on sporting matters as to warrant his announcing himself as a lecturer on the duties of all concerned in the truly British sport of the chasing of the fox. Mr. Jorrocks's antecedents were such as to preclude the possibility of the display of brilliant oratorical powers. His mode of expression—including the absence of the letter "h," where it should be used, and its presence where it should not—was what might have been expected from the retired grocer whose little figure adorns the illustration.

Leech's old friend, Mr. Adams, tells me that a man named Nicholls, Lady Louise Clinton's coachman, was the model for Mr. Jorrocks. Leech never went anywhere, not even to church, without his little sketch-book; and on a special Sunday at Barkway Church, where Lady Clinton had her pew, she was followed by a little man who, after handing her ladyship her books of devotion, took his seat outside the pew, and became an unconscious study for Leech; who in a few minutes transferred an exact likeness to the sketch-book, which was afterwards as exactly reproduced in the "hunting lecture."

A curious reader can study Mr. Jorrocks's lecture in the pages of "Handley Cross." He will there wonder with me how it came about, that so distinguished an audience of aristocratic men, and lovely women, could listen for many minutes to an oration which must have lasted at least two hours, and which ends with the following peroration: "So shall little Spooney jog on rejoicin'! Each succeedin' year shall find him better mounted, and at each fresh deal he will become a wiser and I 'opes a nappier man."

Mr. Jorrocks concluded amidst loud and universal applause.

Leech's mastery of character—unexaggerated, true to nature, without a trace of caricature—can be seen in the foreground figures of this etching. The man standing behind the lady with the lovely profile is a gentleman, though perhaps not a wise one; but what can the beautiful profile find in Mr.

Jorrocks's discourse to amuse or enlighten her? And those pretty creatures in the distance, who certainly seem a little bored, how is it that they did not slip away with their cavaliers behind them, and so leave Mr. Jorrocks to talk about 'unting to 'is 'eart's content?

One of Mr. Jorrocks's sporting friends is Mr. Charley Stobbs, a good-looking young gentleman who finds himself belated after a hard day's hunting. He wanders about an unknown country, darkness comes upon him, and he endeavours in vain to find his way to Handley Cross. "The night was drear and dark, the wind whistled and howled with uncommon keenness, the cutting hail drifted with the sharpness of needles against his face. Horse and rider were equally dispirited," says the chronicler. This free and easy, or, rather uneasy, fox-hunter, determined to seek shelter for the night at the first house he came to, that promised from its appearance a comfortable bed, with, perhaps, an introductory supper. He soon found himself "under the lee of a large house, and having dismounted, and broken his shins against a scraper, he at length discovered a bell-pull in the door-post, which having sounded, the echoing notes from afar proclaimed the size and importance of the mansion." "A little maiden" gave Charley admission, and, with surprising alacrity, provided him with "ham sandwiches, hot water, lemon, nutmeg," etc., to say nothing of a bottle of sherry!

To the common mind the ease with which Mr. Charles Stobbs managed to procure for himself a supper and lodging in a stranger's mansion will be a matter of surprise; in ninety-nine cases out of a hundred he would have met with a very different reception. We rejoice in his success, because it gives us a likeness of his good-looking self, in conjunction with that of one of the prettiest and daintiest waiting-maids ever created by Leech's pencil.

Had I been permitted I should have selected a drawing from "Handley Cross," which heads a chapter called "The Waning Season," not from its subject (which has little interest), but because it is an admirable example of Leech's mastery of landscape. The figure of the old hedger, with his big gauntlets and bill-hook, is as true as possible to nature, well drawn, and perfect in action, as he stoops over the faggots he has collected; but I would call more attention to the drawing of the foreground and distance of the landscape; the stunted tree and the wattled fence in its perspective cunningly going off almost to the horizon—thus leading the eye into space—with its lines so skilfully broken by the leafless trees. The sky, too, though represented by a few lines, composes artistically with the forms in the distance and the rest of the wintry landscape.

With "Ask Mamma"—another of the many sporting books illustrated by Leech—I shall close my selections from that kind of literature for the present.

In the frontispiece of the book, which represents "The Ancestors of our Hero," the female ancestor is such a bewitching creature as to make a reproduction of her in this place irresistible. This charming person is Mrs. William Pringle, *née* Willing, about whose birth, parentage, and education history is silent. Her acquaintance is first made by the reader of "Ask Mamma" in the position of assistant in a milliner's shop, which she soon left for a shop of her own. In this venture Miss Willing failed disastrously, and, leaving dressmaking, she became a lady's-maid in the service of "the beautiful, newly-married Countess Delacey." "It was to the service of the Countess Delacey," says our author, "that Miss Willing was indebted for becoming the wife of Mr. William Pringle." The acquaintance between Miss Willing and Mr. Pringle, which soon ripened into love and marriage, began on the stage-coach, in which Miss Willing was journeying to London to buy dresses for her mistress, the Countess. Alas! it must be confessed that Miss Willing was an unscrupulous adventuress, and Mr. Pringle a very green goose indeed; for when he found Miss Willing installed in the Countess's house in Grosvenor Square, dressed in her mistress's emerald-green velvet costume, he believed her to be, as she represented herself, the mistress of the mansion. A big footman played into Miss Willing's hand, and "my lady'd" her to her heart's content, and to the delight of Mr. Pringle, as the refreshments were supplied to which the victim had been invited. Under the inspiring influence of brandy-and-water Mr. Pringle's love grew apace; and in reply to the lady's prudent inquiries as to his means of keeping her surrounded by the luxury to which she had been accustomed, she was assured that "she should have everything she wanted: a tall footman with good legs, an Arab horse, an Erard harp, a royal pianoforte, a silver tea-urn, a gold coffee pot, a service of gold, *eat gold* if she liked;" and, as he made this declaration, "he dropped upon his salmon-coloured knees, and with his glass of brandy in one hand and hers in the other, looked imploring up at her—a beautiful specimen of heavy sentimentality."

As one looks at the comical figure of Mr. Pringle, it would be difficult to believe that, even with the golden advantages with which he surrounds himself, he could be rendered acceptable to the lovely creature of Leech's fancy; if a finger could not be put upon couples amongst our own acquaintances even more strangely contrasted.

With respect to personal appearance, Mr. Pringle fares better at Leech's hands in a drawing representing a halt in the stage-coach journey to London. The passengers have stopped for refreshment. The coachman attends for his fee. Mr. Pringle, "who was bent upon doing the magnificent, produced a large green-and-gold tasselled purse, almost as big as a stocking, and drew therefrom a great five-shilling piece, which he handed ostentatiously to the man, saying: 'For this lady and me,' just as if she belonged to him."

Here Mr. Pringle fairly resembles a good-looking buck of sixty years ago, and the coachman might have been one of those whom I remember on my own first journey to London, with his "Beg pardon, sir, I've drove you fifty miles," when his fee was less than he expected. The coat of many capes, the red cheeks and redder nose, the action of the man as he holds his hat and whip, are all true to life; here again without the least exaggeration. In composition, light and shade, and general effect, this drawing leaves nothing to wish for. The expression of Miss Willing, as she looks sideways at her victim, should be noted.

Mr. William Pringle did not long enjoy his married life, for his only son (the hero of "Ask Mamma") was but a child, when, "after an inordinate kidney supper, Mr. Pringle was found dead in his chair."

The widow was very rich, and after educating her son regardless of expense, she launched him into high life, and somehow or other brought about an acquaintance between "Billy" and a sporting nobleman, the Earl of Ladythorne. From that time "Ask Mamma" becomes a chronicle of sporting adventure, with which I shall not trouble my reader, beyond the explanation required for the understanding of one or two examples of Leech's work.

The noble Earl of Ladythorne seems to have been a very impressionable personage, in a constant state of suffering from "Cupid's shafts"; and though for some reason or other he objected to hunting ladies, an "equestrian coquette, Miss De Glancey, of half the watering-places in England, and some on the Continent," had but to show herself amongst the field and the noble lord was again transfixed; this time the dart seems to have gone through and through the tender heart, only to be released by an event which occurred shortly afterwards.

It appears that Miss De Glancey's love of hunting was affected, in order to further her designs upon the Earl; she really feared and hated it; and though on the fatal day, which was destined to extinguish her hope of becoming a Countess, she had ridden boldly by the Earl through what he calls "a monstrous fine run," she "found no fun in it at all," and was "monstrous glad when it was over." No sooner was the fox despatched, than the sky darkened, the lightning flashed, the thunder bellowed, and the rain came down in torrents. "Poor Miss De Glancey," says our author, "was ready to sink into the earth." There was nothing for it but to seek the nearest shelter, which seems to have been the Punch Bowl at Rockbeer, in search of which "my lord" and the coquette ride off together. "An opportune flash of lightning so lit up the landscape as to show the clump of large elms at the entrance to Rockbeer." The hard driving rain beats downways and sideways, frontways and backways

—all ways at once. The horses know not which way to duck to evade the storm. In less than a minute Miss De Glancey is as drenched as if she had taken a shower-bath. "The smart hat and feather are annihilated; the dubious frizette falls out; down comes the hair; the *bella-donna*-inspired radiance of her eyes is quenched; the crinoline and wadding dissolve like ice before the fire; and ere *the love-cured Earl* lifts her off her horse at the Punch Bowl at Rockbeer, she has no more shape or figure than an icicle. Indeed, she much resembles one, for the cold sleet, freezing as it fell, has encrusted her in a rich coat of iced lace, causing her saturated garments to cling to her with the utmost pertinacity. A more complete wreck of a belle was perhaps never seen."

"Brief as woman's love," says Shakspeare. That this remark will sometimes apply to man's love cannot be contested, for have we not an example before us in the rapid way in which our noble friend's passion was, so to speak, washed out of him? The love-stricken Earl "cured" by a shower of rain! We ought to be thankful for the downpour, for it was the cause of Leech's drawing, in which the unfortunate coquette is still, under the artist's tender treatment, an elegant creature, with grace and beauty in every line of her bedraggled form. How admirable, too, is the Earl! the rain dripping from the brim of his hat, and with every opportunity for making him ridiculous, he is still dignified, his face and figure noble, as he bends forward to meet the storm. It goes without saying that the horses are admirable in character and action, and that the whole scene exactly realizes a wet and stormy night.

CHAPTER XVIII.

MICHAEL HALLIDAY AND LEECH.

"No man can put more into a picture than there is in himself," says Sir Joshua Reynolds. As an art student I have always felt the force of this aphorism. I would even go further, and add that no man can avoid the disclosure in numberless ways of what "there is in himself" of special mental organization, under the heads of taste, temper, delicacy, honesty, kindliness, and the true and full appreciation of the beauties of nature.

"I cannot see nature as you represent it," someone is said to have remarked to Turner.

"Don't you wish you could?" was the reply.

It is not the subject of a great artist's work that we admire, but the artist's mind as reflected in his subject. Reynolds was fortunate in having for his sitters most of the beauties of the last century, and they were more fortunate still in falling into the hands of a painter who had such intense sympathy with their loveliness—so intense in some instances as to emphasize it somewhat to the sacrifice of individuality. It is what Turner sees in nature that we reverence, producing beauties for us to which we were blind, till they were called up by the spell of the great magician. Heads as fine as any of those painted by Vandyke can be seen any day, but there is no Vandyke to show us the impression they make upon him. Let anyone compare Vandyke's Charles I. with a contemporary rendering of that monarch, and he will feel with me that it is the great painter's power of penetrating the inner man before him, so to speak, added to his sympathy with the melancholy and dignified King, that, combined with his transcendent technical power, enabled him to present to us both the person and the mind of the unfortunate King. The contemporary painters give us but the husk and shell of him.

But of all artists who have reflected themselves in their works, Leech is the best example. Save when his hatred of injustice and oppression is aroused, the man's loving, tender nature, and his honest English, manly character, are apparent in everything he does. As he was to all who knew him well, he shows himself in his treatment of every theme he touches with his pencil. Of his life—quiet, studious, and ever observant—there is little to relate that cannot be gathered from his works. His passionate love of children and childish ways and tricks, his sympathy with beauty in all its forms, his eager participation in manly sports, with numberless other delightful qualities, are part and parcel of the man who was never tired of giving us unconscious revelations of himself in his drawings. Even when a certain amount of ridicule is attached to the principal incidents in the career of a ludicrous personage, we never have a feeling for him approaching contempt.

In the history of Messrs. Briggs and Tom Noddy these gentlemen present themselves in positions of laughable difficulty. Laugh at them we certainly do, but we never despise them; for do they not show the good qualities of courage and fortitude? Tom Noddy is thrown from his horse; nothing daunted, he instantly remounts. He drops his whip; he recovers it: is thrown again, and this time his horse gallops off; but though the little hunter pursues as fast as his little legs can go, the horse has the best of it and escapes. An ordinary being would despair and bemoan his loss; not so Tom Noddy, who gives up the pursuit for a time, and being no doubt a little tired, lights a cigar as he sits upon a stile. When refreshed by tobacco and repose he resumes his horse-chase, and ultimately succeeds in finding the animal in the possession of a rustic, who had amused himself by nearly galloping him to death. Tom Noddy is a delightful little creature; his numerous escapades are plentiful in "Pictures of Life and Character," and will be for all time a hearty, healthy pleasure to all who study them.

Many attempts were made to betray Leech into personality. Subjects were suggested, and offers were made to him, by persons who had real or imaginary grievances, to place well-known public characters in positions ridiculous or contemptible. Those attempts would not have been made if the proposers had known Leech; such suggestions were always rejected, and sometimes in terms very unpleasant to their proposers. I was not aware that Tom Noddy had a prototype until I was informed by my old friend, Mr. Holman Hunt, in a paper of Leech reminiscences, originally intended for this memoir, that Mike Halliday, a man I knew well forty years ago, was the original Tom Noddy. Halliday's figure was intended for an ordinary-sized man, but when Nature had produced his head and shoulders she seemed to have changed her intention, and the rest of his figure was that of a diminutive form, a full foot shorter altogether than an ordinary middle-sized man. When I first became acquainted with Halliday he was a clerk in the House of Lords. "He then," says Holman Hunt, "took to poetry, to love that never found its earthly close, and to our art—for he found time for all. So well did he succeed in picture-making that he once completed an oil-painting of two lovers sitting under a ruined abbey window, habited in contemporary costume, the gentleman intent on taking the size of the lady's marriage-finger."

I remember this picture being exhibited at the Royal Academy in 1856; I thought highly of it, and looked, but in vain, for a repetition of a success so complete as to cause the purchase of the picture by a well-known dealer, who had an engraving made from it, the print meeting with extensive popularity. Halliday's face was a very plain one, but totally unlike that of Tom Noddy: his hair was pale yellow, "a vapoury moustache joining a soft beard, long but sparse whiskers;" he was slightly lame, and altogether an elf-like quaintness in his appearance made him quite a remarkable little figure.

"Leech," says Mr. Hunt, "became intimate with him, and so under many names and ingenious disguises did Leech's public make his acquaintance— Tom Noddy, and a variety of names he figured under. Leech told of an expedition which formed a small party with Halliday one evening in the country, where there was to be a meet with the hounds next morning. As they dined and chatted, the attractions became greater every minute to the cavalier instincts of Halliday's youth. Leech and the others had horses coming, and on inquiry it was found that it would be possible for Mike to find a mount at hand, and so it was pointed out that he could sleep there and have a good day on the morrow.

"'No,' said Halliday, 'I must find a train from town in time to be at the cover.'

"'Why, in the name of mystery—why go to town?' said they all.

"But all was useless—the little man would go, and would come back by a train starting very early from town; and so, to the bewilderment of all, he did. The next morning the friends went to see the train come in. As it stopped, down jumped the little Nimrod, decked out in carefully preserved pink, well-stained cords, with top-boots, and falling over the rim a tassel of ribbons in emulation of Sixteen-stringed Jack, as dandy hunting-men had dressed twenty years before. He was capped with hunting-helmet, and he carried a magnificent riding-whip in hand. Seeing him thus walking and skipping with that outward turn of the feet, which is denominated in horsey parlance 'dishing,' Leech said that with all the desire in the world to treat the matter with supreme seriousness, as Halliday did, it was almost impossible for him to curb his provoked risibility."

Leech, in speaking of Halliday at a party, of which Holman Hunt made one, said:

"Mike is a mine of resource to me. Whenever I am in difficulties I can remember something of him that it is possible to turn into a 'subject'; and," he added earnestly, "I do hope he never recognises the resemblance, for I often put some point to prevent recognition."

The surprise at this innocence made the whole table burst into laughter, but in undeceiving Leech we were able to assure him that Halliday was by no means pained by the darts which had struck him; that he wore them proudly as decorations, and so disarmed the ill-nature that might be disposed to take advantage of the chance. He often achieved this by drawing the attention of his visitors to the last addition to his gallery of *Punch* portraits, exhibited on the walls of his studio.

It must have been from some peculiarity of dress or manner, to which Halliday's attention was called by "a candid friend," that he discovered that in drawing Tom Noddy Leech "had him in his eye"; for, as I said before, his face was as unlike that of Tom Noddy as Leech's own face was unlike the round, good-humoured physiognomy of Mr. Briggs, though some of the escapades of Briggs had their origin in Leech's personal experiences: a happy accident to the roof of Leech's house, and the noise and varied troubles caused in repairing it, was the suggestion of the famous scene of the Briggs disaster; and it was Leech himself who was caught by the leg by a policeman as— finding his front door blocked by scaffolding—he was attempting to enter in what that functionary considered a burglarious manner.

Leech was more fortunate than another artist of my acquaintance, for the officer listened to his explanation of the unusual way of entering his house, and, believing the statement, assisted him to "make himself at home." But my other friend, who had been "dining," finding something the matter with his latch-key—for do what he would he could not induce it to perform its usual office—mounted his area railings, and would very likely have fallen into the area if he had not been stopped by a policeman. The artist's attempts to explain his position were either incomprehensible by the officer, or they were not believed, for he was taken to the station and locked up for the night.

Leech gives us no hint by which we might guess in what condition of life the immortal Briggs made the fortune that enabled him to retire to his comfortable home in Bayswater; whatever his pursuit may have been, the taste for sport of every kind must have possessed the prosperous gentleman, to be indulged to the full—happily for us—when he had achieved independence.

Leech's powers are seen in their highest development in the Briggs drawings. Mr. Briggs is unfortunate in respect of horseflesh; the animals he selects are none of them free from vice, and in their various—and often successful— attempts to unseat their rider, they give the artist opportunities of showing his power of representing almost every action of which the horse is capable in the indulgence of that propensity. The enterprising sportsman chases the fox, coming in at the death, or soon after it—anyway, in time to give the huntsman half-a-sovereign for the brush, only he must "say nothing about it." He rides steeplechases, and though he is half drowned in a water-jump, and suffers other hindrances, he wins the race.

But it is in the shooting and fishing exploits that the sportsman and his illustrator shine most. Among so many triumphs of art and sportsmanship, it is difficult to say which of the many excellent examples is to be preferred; all are admirable, but I think the one I have chosen for illustration is my favourite. Mr. Briggs is deer-stalking, and though he occasionally suffers, even to prostration, from the heat of the weather, and the difficulties presented by hills, rocks, and heather, he really enjoys creeping and hiding with his gillies, until the royal hart, which the forester has seen through his glass, is well within rifle shot. He fires, misses; and behold the result!

**"After aiming for a Quarter of an Hour, Mr. B. fires both his Barrels
and misses!! Tableau: the Forester's Anguish."**

In expression, drawing, character, and action, the figure of the forester is
perfect; there is a tragic grandeur in the pose that would be appropriate in the
gravest scene of misfortune. Poor Mr. Briggs plainly shows us that he not
only suffers from the mortification of having missed so splendid an
opportunity of distinguishing himself, but also from the misery his mishap has
inflicted upon the forester. The skilful way in which this drawing is composed
—the three figures separated from each other presenting a difficult problem to
the artist—excites one's admiration. Without the connecting links afforded by
the forms in the landscape, and the lines made by the dogs in the leash, held
by the young gilly, the figures would be unpleasantly separated. As it is, with
the masterly effect of light and shadow, this drawing is above all criticism.

My elderly readers may remember a certain Mr. Rarey, an American, I think,
who "took the town" by his horse-taming feats. A horse named Cruiser, which
was in the habit of indulging in every wickedness that could disgrace a horse,
became docile under the Rarey treatment. The tamer's method was a profound
secret; he allowed no one to witness the working of the charm by which a
furious animal was changed into lamb-like meekness. In Cruiser's case, what
was certain was, that a creature unapproachable without risk to limb and life,
was transformed to such an extent that a child might—and did—ride him.

In a number of admirably humorous drawings, Leech pictures Mr. Briggs,
who comes to grief in all his attempts to emulate Mr. Rarey. He evidently

does not possess the secret, and though we laugh over his failures, we respect the courage which led to them. "Mr. Briggs tries his shooting pony" is an inimitable drawing. Mr. B. has no doubt been assured that the pony will take no more notice of a gun when fired from his back than "if you was to whistle a tune as you was riding of him." In perfect confidence in the truthfulness of the dealer's assurance, Mr. Briggs fires. The pony instantly flies, rather than gallops, away—without, however, unseating Mr. Briggs, who clings to the saddle, clutching his gun still smoking from the recent discharge.

Mr. Briggs goes to Scotland after salmon, as well as deer and grouse. As a fisherman he is more successful with the rod than he was as a deer-stalker with the gun. A huge salmon, for which "he would not take a guinea a pound," rewards him for a long and desperate struggle, in which he encounters obstacles in the shape of the slippery rocks and deep-water holes that distinguish a Highland river.

In Scottish scenery Leech is as much at home as he is in the turnip-field or the covert. No praise can be too extravagant for all the backgrounds that form so perfect a setting for the gem-like figures of Mr. Briggs. Nor must his attendants be forgotten. Witness the difference of character, so completely marked, between the snuff-taking bearer of the "gaff," with his Scotch bonnet, and the forester in his kilt, who so pathetically mourns Mr. Briggs' failure, and who afterwards makes him "free of the forest" by smearing his face with the blood of a stag which has died by the accidental discharge of his gun.

During the quarter of a century of Leech's work, the British public had its crazes—Bloomerism, crinoline, spirit-rapping, and other less dangerous absurdities than the last, seized upon the minds of large portions of the people, to be thrown aside and replaced by other ridiculous fancies. Even games, after a time, seem to pall upon the players: cricket, happily, bids fair to be perennial; but croquet, once so fashionable, is no more. When one looks at Leech's drawings, in which crinolines figure so prominently, it is really difficult to believe that the artist has not exaggerated a frightful fashion; from observation I can assure a doubter that Leech has frequently under, rather than over, done the swell of those voluminous skirts. Of course, whenever they are permitted to do so, servants will imitate their masters and mistresses, and it was by no means uncommon for the ribs of a housemaid's crinoline to assert themselves through the outer skirt, as we see in some of Leech's drawings.

I would draw attention to the opposite, or antithesis, of this. In some of the cuts, prior, I think, to the "crinoline mania," Leech's delightful girls wear jackets of a form that follows the lines of nature, and of a very picturesque shape. These have a very short reign, being discarded in their turn by that Goddess of Fashion, the dressmaker, for "something new" and outrageous.

There is amongst the "Pictures of Life and Character" a drawing of a dinner-party in which the male guests are so hidden and covered by ladies' crinolines that their heads and a small portion of their shoulders only are visible. How the gentlemen's hands are to be used in the consumption of their dinners is left to the imagination of the beholder, and of the sufferers.

For the unexaggerated truth of this print I, who write, can vouch; for have I not again and again been obliged to solve the difficulty of using my knife and fork? In spite of the attacks upon it, crinoline had its day—and far too long a day it was.

The Bloomer costume—a Yankee invention—made but a feeble struggle for existence, though it had many advocates, notably a *belle Americaine*, one of whose lectures at the Hanover Square rooms I had the curiosity to attend. The lady wore a red velvet overcoat and loose trousers, a broad-brimmed black hat and feather, and looked and talked like a pretty boy.

Bloomerism afforded Leech many opportunities of showing that his pencil could invest eccentricity with beauty. A study of the Bloomer sketches will also show that the attempt to adopt the manly dress was, in his estimation, an insidious attempt to usurp manly work and offices. In proof of this see the charming Bloomer omnibus-conductor, who is threatened by an elderly male passenger with a summons for abusive language; or the group of Bloomer police, who fly from a riotous mob instead of arresting the ringleaders. Look at her again as "the man at the wheel" who must not be "spoken to." Those who have suffered from sea-sickness will see by the expression of the Bloomer's countenance why she should not be spoken to, and what the effect of conversation under the circumstances would most probably be. Leech gave his imagination full play in this fruitful theme. Granting the assumption of the masculine dress, he sees no reason why a proposal should not be made by the female lover instead of the male. Why, he seems to ask, should the gentleman have to undergo that terrible ordeal?

I advise my reader to seek in "Pictures of Life and Character" for a drawing of an elopement in which the positions of the principals are reversed. It is the lady who is pouring words of passionate persuasion into the ears of her frightened and half-reluctant lover, as he looks back at the home he is leaving for ever; she almost drags him to the carriage which is to bear the happy pair away to Gretna Green.

Spirit-rapping, table-turning, and the rest of it, fare badly at the hands of Leech. Happy was the thought that possessed him when, by a touch of his magic pencil, he changed the heads of a seance-party into those of geese. And how admirably humorous is the drawing in which furniture starts into life at the bidding of a medium, to the astonishment and dismay of the housemaid!

Hats were supposed to "turn about and wheel about" under the influence of encircled hands round the brims. It would be a mistake to suppose that the handsome Guardsman who, with the assistance of the fingers of those pretty creatures, so patiently waits for the hat to move, has either the expectation or the desire that the experiment will be successful. No, he greatly enjoys the situation, and is eager to prolong it for any unreasonable time.

Here I cannot resist interposing a little anecdote of an experience of which I should like to have an explanation by the spiritualists. The incident took place on one of the many occasions when I served as a member of the dreaded Hanging Committee of the Royal Academy. As is well known, the Academicians have a vast variety of works of art offered for exhibition, perpetrated, as a rule, by human hands. But there is no rule without an exception, and it was my fate to witness the exception in the form of pictures painted by spirits, and sent for exhibition by their thrice-blessed proprietor. These were very striking works indeed. At first sight they looked like masses of many-coloured weeds, very weird vegetation, unlike anything "in heaven above or on the earth beneath." On nearer inspection, some childishly-drawn, half-naked figures were discernible amongst the weeds, intended to represent spiritual forms of departed friends, probably, who had been changed into these unfortunate figures. These works received our most careful examination, created laughter, and were rejected. Now, I respectfully ask what the spirits were about thus to subject themselves and their doings to the ignorant ribaldry of the Academicians? They must have known that we were in a state of darkest unbelief, and the least they could have done was to warn the owner of these works of their certain fate at our hands, and thus have saved him the trouble of sending them to Burlington House, to say nothing of the expense of the handsome frames in which they were enshrined. "I pause for a reply."

Archery and croquet afforded Leech opportunities for the display of beauty in many forms. His lady-archers are bewitching creatures, their male competitors always manly, graceful gentlemen. The pursuit of both amusements offered chances of love-making and flirtation, of which full advantage is sometimes taken; indeed, in one instance we see a game of croquet stopped altogether by a couple who find an interchange of—shall we say vows?—more interesting than the game; a feeling which, judging from the other players, is by no means shared.

Leech seems to have left no phase of human life and character untouched: whether he deals with the aristocrat or the plebeian, the Duchess or the beggar, the very poor or the very rich, the beautiful or the ugly, he is ever true to Nature; turning away from our vices, dealing lovingly with us in all ways, touching our follies lightly, humorously, and always good-naturedly—in short, invariably reflecting in his work his own disposition to what is pure, manly, and true.

CHAPTER XIX.

THOMAS HOOD AND LEECH.

The difficulty of gauging public taste in matters literary and artistic can be proved by numberless examples. How often does the manager of a theatre place in trembling anxiety a piece before his audience which afterwards runs for hundreds of nights! "Our Boys" has had a long life upon the stage; but so doubtful was everyone connected with its production of its living for one night even, that another play was held in readiness to take the place of the damned one. Books that have made reputations for their authors have been refused by publisher after publisher. Engravings run the same perilous course. Print-sellers, from long experience of public wants, should know what will satisfy them; but they seem to find the difficulty that befalls publishers and the managers of theatres.

Many years ago a very pretty servant-maid became a part of my household. I induced her to sit for me, having noticed the graceful way in which her various duties were performed; and I made a half-length figure of her carrying a silver salver, on which was a decanter, thinking that the contrast between the silver, glass, and a pretty gray dress would make an effective scheme of colour. The picture was beautifully engraved by Holl, and offered for publication by a friend, who bought it, to one of the most experienced print-sellers in London. To please my friend, to whom the print-seller was under great obligation, he bought the right of publication; but having no faith in its success, my pretty servant was passed on—at a sacrifice—to another print-seller, and she afterwards found great favour with the public, and was highly remunerative to her proprietor, under the name and title of "Sherry, sir?" This title was the "happy thought" of the print-seller, who, on my remonstrating with him for vulgarizing my picture, informed me that the title had been the sole cause of the success of the engraving.

A print was published many years ago of three chorister boys in surplice and cassock, who, with open mouths and upturned eyes, are supposed to be singing. In a moment of inspiration the artist, who, I believe, was also the engraver, christened his subject, "We praise Thee, O Lord!" and then offered it at most of the principal print-shops in London, where it was invariably refused. The artist published "We praise Thee," etc., himself, and, I was told, made more than two thousand pounds by it.

All this is introductory to the most astonishing example that could be conceived of the fallacy of what I may call expert opinion, on literary merit and public taste.

I am not sure of the precise date, but I think it was about 1848 or 1849 that Hood's "Song of the Shirt" appeared in *Punch*. There is, or was, a letter in existence from Hood to Mark Lemon, then editor of *Punch*, in which the writer tells his friend he has enclosed a poem that he may publish in *Punch* if he likes; but he "most likely won't like," and refuse it, as the publishers, one and all, to whom it has been offered, had done without hesitation. "In that case," said Hood, "tear it up, and put it in the waste-paper-basket; for I am sick of the sight of it." This was the "Song of the Shirt," one of the most powerful, touching, and pathetic poems in the English language.

My old friend, Willert Beale, whose recently-published "Light of Other Days" has charmed so many readers, sends me the following account of the introduction of the "Song of the Shirt" into *Punch*:

"Mark Lemon" (then editor of *Punch*) "was looking over the immense heap of *Punch* letters on his desk, when he opened one enclosing a poem, which the writer said had been rejected by three contemporaries, and if unavailable for *Punch*, he begged the editor, whom he knew but slightly, to consign the paper to his waste-basket, as he was sick of the sight of it. The poem was signed 'Tom Hood,' and entitled 'The Song of the Shirt,' now so famous among us all. Of a totally different character to anything that had previously appeared in the pages of *Punch*, most of the staff were dead set against the insertion of it; but Mark Lemon, whose quick appreciation of its merits made him unwilling to let so valuable a prize slip from his grasp, over-ruled all objections with quiet though firm determination, and brought it before the public through the medium of *Punch*. The insertion *trebled* the sale of the number. Mark Lemon was always very proud of this success, which was certainly attributable to his efforts.

"'Hood wants but one thing to make him famous,' he used to say, 'and that is death.'

"His words were verified, for in poverty and comparative obscurity died one of England's cleverest men."

In 1849 some very painful disclosures were made in the Metropolitan police-courts, when it appeared "that numbers of poor sempstresses were paid by the slop-sellers only three-halfpence for making a shirt, and in proportion for other articles of ready-made clothing." In all probability these disclosures suggested the "Song of the Shirt," as they assuredly did the charming designs by Leech, called "Pin-Money" and "Needle-Money." It seems to me almost an impertinence for a commentator on such admirable designs as these to point out the beauties so palpable to all who look at them. We sympathize with each of these classes of beings, for they are both the results of conditions that they have done nothing to create. It is certain that one of them is miserable, and it is by no means sure that the lovely girl's pin-money brings happiness with it.

There was everything in the shape of similarity of thought and feeling to have brought Leech and Hood into intimacy, but I doubt if they ever saw much of each other. Hood's comparatively premature death, preceded by much sickness and seclusion, took place while Leech was far from the position in public estimation that he afterwards reached. In proof of similarity of humour I give the following note from Hood to Dickens:

> "17, Elm Tree Road, 1841,
> *Saturday.*

"DEAR DICKENS,

"As you are going to America, and have kindly offered to execute any little commission for me, pray, if it be not too much trouble, try to get me an autograph of Sandy Hook's. I have Theodore's.

> "Yours very truly,
>
> > "THOS. HOOD.

"My boy does *not* wait for an answer."

"Miss Kilmansegg and her Precious Leg: a Golden Legend," is perhaps one of the best, as it is certainly the longest, of Hood's poems, remarkable, indeed, for its puns and ingenious play upon words, its felicitous rhyming, and its underlying moral. Miss Kilmansegg was born with a golden spoon in her mouth, and her condition is shown in the charming drawing with which Leech illustrates the following lines:

"What wide reverses of fate are there!
  Whilst Margaret, charmed by the Bulbul rare,
    In a Garden of Gull reposes,
  Poor Peggy hawks nosegays from street to street,
  Till—think of that, who find life so sweet!—
    She hates the smell of roses!

"WHAT WIDE REVERSES OF FATE ARE THERE!"

"Not so with the infant Kilmansegg—
  She was not born to steal or beg,
    Or gather cresses in ditches;
  To plait the straw, or bind the shoe,
  Or sit all day to hem and sew,
  As females must—and not a few!—
    To fill their insides with stitches."

The christening of the golden child was an affair so splendid as to tax the poet's invention for tropes and figures worthy of the occasion:

"Gold! and gold! and nothing but gold!
  The same auriferous shine behold
    Wherever the eye could settle!
  On the walls—the sideboard—the ceiling—sky—,
  On the gorgeous footmen standing by,
  In coats to delight a miner's eye
    With seams of precious metal.

"Gold! and gold! and besides the gold,

The very robe of the infant told
A tale of wealth in every fold—
   It lapped her like a vapour!
So fine! so thin! the mind at a loss,
Could compare it to nothing except a cross
   Of cobweb with banknote paper."

Powerful as the poet's imagination shows in these glittering rhymes, it fails him in his endeavour to find a prefix in the form of a name worthy of accompanying Kilmansegg. He says:

"Then the babe was crossed and blessed amain,
   But instead of Kate, or Ann, or Jane,
      Which the humbler female endorses—
Instead of one name, as some people prefix,
Kilmansegg went at the tails of six,
   Like a carriage of state with its horses."

The names, therefore, are left to the imagination of the reader, who may learn, if he will, some particulars of the nameless Kilmansegg's childhood:

"Turn we to little Miss Kilmansegg,
   Cutting her first little toothy-peg
      With a fifty-guinea coral—
        A peg upon which
        About poor and rich
   Reflection might hang on a moral.

"Born in wealth, and wealthily nursed,
   Capp'd, papp'd, napp'd, and lapp'd from the first
      On the knees of Prodigality,
Her childhood was one eternal round
Of the game of going on Tiddler's ground,
   Picking up gold in reality.

*   *   *   *   *

"Gold! and gold! 'twas the burden still!
   To gain the heiress's early goodwill
      There was much corruption and bribery.
The yearly cost of her golden toys
Would have given half London's charity boys
And charity girls the annual joys
   Of a holiday dinner at Highbury."

The kind of education permitted to this unfortunate heiress may be gathered from the following extracts:

"Long before her A B and C
  They had taught her by heart her £ s. d.,
    And as how she was born a great heiress;
  And as sure as London was made of bricks
  My Lord would ask her the day to fix
  To ride in a fine gilt coach and six,
    Like her Worship the Lady Mayoress.

"The very metal of merit they told,
  And praised her for being as 'good as gold'!
    Till she grew as a peacock haughty;
  Of money they talked the whole day round,
  And weighed desert like grapes, by the pound,
  Till she had an idea from the very sound
    That people with naught were naughty.

"Gold! still gold....
  Gold ran in her thoughts and filled her brain,
  She was golden-headed, like Peter's cane,
    With which he walked behind her."

MISS KILMANSEGG.

Leech's drawings which decorate "Miss Kilmansegg" display his appreciation of beauty and character, and are, in some examples, of great artistic excellence—notably in the portrait of the foreign gentleman who became the husband of the heiress. Some of them are, of course, deficient in the artistic qualities with which his long practice enabled him to enrich his latest work.

My space will not permit of my making many extracts from Hood's admirable work—only, indeed, so far as to explain Leech's drawings; but to those of my readers who make Miss Kilmansegg's acquaintance for the first time in these pages, I heartily recommend a perusal of the poem, and envy them the pleasure they will find in reading it.

Of course Miss Kilmansegg

"… learnt to sing and to dance,
To sit on a horse although he should prance,
And to speak a French not spoken in France
 Any more than at Babel's building."

The steed was a thoroughbred of great spirit—

"A regular thoroughbred Irish horse,
 And he ran away, as a matter of course,
  With a girl worth her weight in guineas."

I think it would be very difficult to find a description of any event in any book to equal Hood's account of the mad career of the Irish horse and its unfortunate rider:

"Away went the horse in the madness of fright,
 And away went the horsewoman mocking the sight;
 Was yonder blue flash a flash of blue light,
  Or only the flash of her habit?

"Away she flies, and the groom behind"—

encountering all the perils of London streets, till the inevitable catastrophe takes place:

"On and on! still frightfully fast!
 Dover Street, Bond Street, all are past! But—yes—no—yes!—
they're down at last!

*   *   *   *   *

   There's a shriek and a sob
   And the dense dark mob
Like a billow closes around them!
     'She breathes!'

       'She don't'
       'She'll recover!'
       'She won't.'
  'She's stirring! she's living by Nemesis!'
Gold, still gold, on counter and shelf,
Golden dishes as plenty as delf,
Miss Kilmansegg's coming again to herself
    On an opulent goldsmith's premises!"

The heiress recovers; but, alas! in her fall she broke her leg, and as "the limb was doomed it couldn't be saved." A substitute must be found. Of what, then, shall the "proxy limb" be made?

"She couldn't—she shouldn't—she wouldn't have wood!
  Nor a leg of cork, if she never stood;
  And she swore an oath, or something as good,
    The proxy limb should be golden!

So a leg was made in a comely mould
Of gold—fine virgin, glittering gold—
    As solid as man could make it;
Solid in foot, and calf, and shank,
A prodigious sum of money it sank;
In fact 'twas a Branch of the family Bank,
    And no easy matter to break it."

The golden leg became the talk of the town, kicking away all other attractions. The new novel, the new murder, even "wild Irish riots and rum-pusses," were neglected; in fact, "the leg was in everybody's mouth," and a grand fancy ball was given at the Kilmansegg mansion to celebrate the heiress's recovery, as well as to exhibit the golden leg. All the world and his wife worship at the golden shrine:

"In they go—in jackets, and cloaks,
  Plumes and bonnets, turbans and tokes,
    As if to a congress of nations:
Greeks and Malays, with daggers and dirks,
Spaniards and Jews, Chinese and Turks—
Some like original foreign works,
    But mostly like bad translations.

*   *   *   *   *

But where—where—where? with one accord
Cried Moses and Mufti, Jack and my Lord,
  Wang-Fong and Il Bondacani—

When slow and heavy, and dead as a dump,
They heard a foot begin to stump,
                    Thump! lump!
                    Lump! thump!
    Like the spectre in 'Don Giovanni!'

"And lo! the heiress, Miss Kilmansegg,
  With her splendid, brilliant, beautiful leg,
     In the garb of a Goddess olden—
  Like chaste Diana going to hunt
  With a golden spear—which of course was blunt,
  And a tunic looped up to a gem in front,
     To show the leg was golden."

The fancy ball was a great success, and at supper—which the poet describes in glowing language—the heiress's health was proposed:

                "'Miss Kilmansegg,
                    Full glasses I beg.
  Miss Kilmansegg and her Precious Leg!'
     And away went the bottle careering!
  Wine in bumpers! and shouts in peals!
  Till the clown didn't know his head from his heels,
  The Mussulman's eyes danced two-some reels,
     And the Quaker was hoarse with cheering!"

The party being over, and the last guest gone, Miss Kilmansegg went to bed and to dream:

"Miss Kilmansegg took off her leg
  And laid it down like a cribbage-peg,
     For the rout was done and the riot;
  The square was hushed, not a sound was heard
  The sky was gray, and no creature stirr'd
  Except one little precocious bird
     That chirped—and then was quiet.

*   *   *   *   *

"And then on the bed her frame she cast,
  The time for repose had come at last;
  But long, long after the storm is past
     Rolls the turbid, turbulent billow."

She dreams:

"Gold! she saw at her golden foot

105

The Peer whose tree has an olden root;
The Proud, the Great, the Learned to boot,
    The handsome, the gay, and the witty—
The man of Science—of Arms—of Art,
The man who deals but at Pleasure's mart,
    And the man who deals in the City."

The poet now rhymes delightfully of the time—the perilous time—when a choice has to be made of a partner in life for the heiress. The dream was realized so far as regards the number of her suitors, for—

        "to tell the rigid truth,
Her favour was sought by Age and Youth,
    For the prey will find a prowler!
She was followed, flattered, courted, address'd,
Woo'd and coo'd and wheedl'd, and press'd
By suitors from North, South, East, and West,
    Like that Heiress in song, 'Tibbie Fowler.'"

The *embarras de choix* resulted, as often happens, in the selection of the worst of the group:

"A foreign Count—who came incog.
  Not under a cloud, but under a fog,
    In a Calais packet's fore-cabin,

To charm some lady British-born,
With his eyes as black as the fruit of the thorn,
And his hooky nose, and his beard half shorn,
    Like a half-converted Rabbin.

*   *   *   *   *

"He was dressed like one of the glorious trade—
  At least, when Glory is off parade—
With a stock, and a frock, well trimmed with braid,
And frogs—that went a-wooing."

"THE FOREIGN COUNT."

He could

"act the tender, and do the cruel;
For amongst his other killing parts,
He had broken a brace of female hearts,
    And murdered three men in a duel.

"Savage at heart, and false of tongue;
  Subtle with age, and smooth to the young,
    Like a snake in his coiling and curling,
  Such was the Count—to give him a niche—
Who came to court that heiress rich,
And knelt at her foot—one needn't say which—
    Besieging her Castle of *Sterling*."

In the whole range of Leech's art, no more subtle realization of character can be found than this wonderful drawing presents; in every touch, in every line, can be read the savage brutality of the man to whom the happiness of Hood's poor rich heroine is confided. How evident is "the trail of the serpent" over features not unhandsome! The love that could fail to be warned by such a face must be blind indeed. The poet's comments, and the contrast he shows between the lots of those who "marry for money" and those in whom simple and true love have been the guiding stars, are delightful. I add an example:

"But, oh! the love that gold must crown!
 Better, better, the love of the clown,
 Who admires his lass in her Sunday gown,
     As if all the fairies had dressed her!
 Whose brain to no crooked thought gives birth,
 Except that he never will part on earth
     With his truelove's crooked tester!

"Alas! for the love that's linked with gold,
 Better, better a thousand times told—
     More honest and happy and laudable,
 The downright loving of pretty Ciss,
 Who wipes her lips, though there's nothing amiss,
 And takes a kiss, and gives a kiss,
     In which her heart is audible."

The Count has been accepted; he has presented his betrothed

"With a miniature sketch of his hooky nose,
 And his dear dark eyes as black as sloes,
 And his beard and whiskers as black as those.
     The lady's consent he requited:
 And instead of the lock that lovers beg,
 The Count received from Miss Kilmansegg
 A model, in small, of her precious leg—
     And so the couple were plighted!"

But a short time probably elapsed between the betrothal and the marriage, which was solemnized, with golden splendour, of course, at St. James's Church. Thus the poet sings:

"'Twas morn—a most auspicious one!
 From the golden east, the golden sun
 Came forth his glorious race to run
     Through clouds of most splendid tinges;
 Clouds that had lately slept in shade,
         But now seemed made
         Of gold brocade,
     With magnificent gold fringes.

* * * * *

"In short, 'twas the year's most golden day,
 By mortals called the first of May,

108

When Miss Kilmansegg,
       Of the golden leg
    With a golden ring was married.

*   *   *   *   *

"And then to see the groom! the Count
  With Foreign Orders to such an amount,
     And whiskers so wild—nay, bestial;
  He seemed to have borrowed the shaggy hair,
  As well as the stars, of the Polar Bear,
     To make him look celestial!"

Of course the church was crowded inside and out,

"For next to that interesting job,
  The hanging of Jack, or Bill, or Bob,
  There's nothing that draws a London mob
     As the noosing of very rich people.

*   *   *   *   *

"And then, great Jove! the struggle, the crush,
  The screams, the heaving, the awful rush,
     The swearing, the tearing, the fighting;
  The hats and bonnets, smashed like an egg,
  To catch a glimpse of the golden leg,
  Which between the steps and Miss Kilmansegg
     Was fully displayed in alighting.

*   *   *   *   *

"But although a magnificent veil she wore,
  Such as never was seen before,
  In case of blushes, she blushed no more
     Than George the First on a guinea!

*   *   *   *   *

"Bravely she shone—and shone the more,
  As she sailed through the crowd of squalid and poor,
     Thief, beggar, and tatterdemalion;
  Led by the Count, with his sloe-black eyes,
  Bright with triumph, and some surprise,
  Like Anson, in making sure of his prize,
     The famous Mexican galleon.

*   *   *   *   *

"Six 'Handsome Fortunes,' all in white,
  Came to help the marriage rite,
    And rehearse their own hymeneals;
  And then the bright procession to close,
  They were followed by just as many beaux—
    Quite fine enough for ideals.

"And how did the bride perform her part?
  Like any bride who is cold at heart,
    Mere snow with the ice's glitter;
  What but a life of winter for her?
  Bright but chilly, alive without stir,
  So splendidly comfortless, just like a fir
    When the frost is severe and bitter.

"Yet wedlock's an awful thing!
  'Tis something like that feat in the ring
    Which requires good nerve to do it,
      When one of a 'grand equestrian troop'
      Makes a jump at a gilded hoop,
        Not certain at all
        Of what may befall
    After his getting through it.

"Such were the future of man and wife,
  Whose bale or bliss to the end of life
    A few short words were to settle:
      Wilt thou have this woman?
        I will—and then,
      Wilt thou have this man?
        I will, and Amen——
And those two were one flesh in the angels' ken,
  Except one leg—that was metal."

—"Wilt thou have this Woman?"

Here we have the Count in profile, only more agreeable because the view affords less of his villainous face.

I confess I am disappointed with Leech's rendering of Miss Kilmansegg. I cannot see why she should be deprived of a portion of the sympathy one always feels for "beauty in distress." Why should she be represented as the commonplace, red-nosed creature who plays the part of the bride in Leech's drawing? To be sure, the contrast she affords to the sweet little bridesmaid behind her heightens that young lady's attractions; but I cannot help thinking the heiress is hardly treated.

I pass over the wedding-breakfast, which was composed of everything in season, and of much that was out of it—

"For wealthy palates there be that scout
  What is *in* season for what is *out*,
    And prefer all precocious savour;
  For instance, early green peas, of the sort
  That costs some four or five guineas a quart,
    Where *mint* is the principal flavour."

The inevitable honeymoon follows—

"To the loving a bright and constant sphere

111

That makes earth's commonest scenes appear
    All poetic, romantic, and tender;
Hanging with jewels a cabbage-stump,
And investing a common post or a pump,
A currant-bush or a gooseberry clump,
    With a halo of dream-like splendour."

"Oh, happy, happy, thrice happy state,
When such a bright planet governs the fate
    Of a pair of united lovers!
Tis theirs, in spite of the serpent's hiss,
To enjoy the pure primeval kiss,
With as much of the old original bliss
    As mortality ever recovers."

"LOVE AT THE BOARD."

I hope my readers will agree with me, that amongst the pleasures we receive from this delightful poem, one of the greatest is the charming little sketch which it has suggested to Leech in these two happy lovers, completely wrapped up in each other, with love in the cottage, at the board, and all about them.

But the Kilmansegg moon!

"Now, the Kilmansegg moon, it must be told,
    Though instead of silver it tipped with gold,

Shone rather wan, and distant, and cold;
    And before its days were thirty,
Such gloomy clouds began to collect,
With an ominous ring of ill-effect,
As gave but too much cause to expect
    Such weather as seamen call dirty.

"She hated lanes, she hated fields,
  She hated all that the country yields,
    And barely knew turnips from clover;
She hated walking in any shape,
And a country stile was an awkward scrape,
Without the bribe of a mob to gape
    At the leg in clambering over.

"Gold, still gold, her standard of old—
  All pastoral joys were tried by gold,
    Or by fancies golden and crural,
Till ere she had passed one week unblest
As her agricultural uncle's guest,
Her mind was made up and fully imprest
    That felicity could not be rural."

And the Count?

"To the snow-white lambs at play,
  And all the scents and sights of May,
    And the birds that warbled their passion,
His ears, and dark eyes, and decided nose,
Were as deaf, and as blind, and as dull as those
That overlook the Bouquet de Rose,
      The Huile Antique,
      And Parfum Unique,
In a Barber's Temple of Fashion.

"And yet had that fault been his only one,
  The pair might have had few quarrels or none,
    For their tastes thus far were in common;
But faults he had that a haughty bride
With a golden leg could hardly abide—
Faults that would even have roused the pride
    Of a far less metalsome woman.

*   *   *   *   *

"He left her, in spite of her tender regards,

And those loving murmurs described by bards,
For the rattling of dice and the shuffling of cards
   And the poking of balls into pockets.

"Moreover, he loved the deepest stake
  And the heaviest bets the players would make,
    And he drank—the reverse of sparely!
And he used strange curses that made her fret;
And when he played with herself at picquet,
    She found to her cost—
    For she always lost—
  That the Count did not count quite fairly.

"And then came dark mistrust and doubt,
  Gathered by worming his secrets out,
    And slips in his conversation—
Fears which all her peace destroyed,
That his title was null, his coffers were void,
And his French château was in Spain, or enjoyed
    The most airy of situations.

"But still his heart—if he had such a part—
She—only she—might possess his heart,
    And hold her affections in fetters.
Alas! that hope, like a crazy ship,
Was forced its anchor and cable to slip
When, seduced by her fears, she took a dip
    In his private papers and letters—

"Letters that told of dangerous leagues,
  And notes that hinted as many intrigues
    As the Count's in the 'Barber of Seville.'
In short, such mysteries came to light
That the Countess-bride, on the thirtieth night,
Woke and started up in a fright,
And kicked and screamed with all her might,
And finally fainted away outright,
    For she dreamt she had married the Devil!"

In short, poor Miss Kilmansegg, or, rather, the "Golden Countess," was
utterly wretched:

"Her cheek is pale, and her eye is dim,
  And downward cast, yet not at the limb
    Once the centre of all speculation;

But downward drooping in comfort's dearth,
As gloomy thoughts are drawn to the earth—
Whence human sorrows derive their birth—
    By a moral gravitation.

"How blessed the heart that has a friend
  A sympathizing ear to lend
    To troubles too great to smother!
  But friend or gossip she had none
  To hear the vile deeds the Count had done,
  How night after night he rambled;
  And how she learned by sad degrees
  That he drank and smoked, and, worse than these,
    That he 'swindled, intrigued, and gambled'!

*   *   *   *   *

"He brought *strange* gentlemen home to dine
  That he said were in the Fancy Line,—
  And they fancied spirits instead of wine,
  And called her lap-dog 'Wenus.'"

Leech has pretty well marked the profession of the "strange gentlemen" in this admirable drawing; their attitudes, the cut of their clothes, the character in their figures, to say nothing of the sticking-plaster on a face that could belong to no one but a "fighting man," sufficiently proclaim their habits. The figure of the Count is tragic in its intensity of drunken self-abandonment.

A leg of solid gold would, no doubt, if turned into cash, represent a large sum of money. It seems to have been the determination of the Countess, while still Miss Kilmansegg, to have reserved to herself all rights over the golden leg, for that auriferous limb was settled, as well as fixed upon herself, to be disposed of by will or otherwise, as she pleased. Says the poet:

"So the Countess, then Miss Kilmansegg,
  At her marriage refused to stir a peg
Till her lawyers had fastened on her leg,
  As fast as the law could tie it."

Means which seem illimitable very speedily vanish when they fall into the hands of such people as the foreign Count. It was said of a famous *roué* of the last century that he "practised every vice except prodigality and hypocrisy— his insatiable avarice exempted him from the first, and his matchless impudence from the second." Our Count seems to have surpassed his prototype, whose "impudence" may not have been of the brutal character from which the poor Countess suffered; whilst a slight dash of avarice might have prevented the golden leg from being all that was left of her golden fortune.

The following lines eloquently describe the Count's state of mind after his orgies:

"And then how wildly he used to stare,
  And shake his fist at nothing, and swear,
  And pluck by the handful his shaggy hair,
  Till he looked like a study of Giant Despair
    For a new edition of Bunyan!

"For dice will run the contrary way,
  As is well known to all who play,
    And cards will conspire as in treason."

At all events, cards, dice, and other expensive amusements had so reduced the Count that he had not a leg to stand upon, except his wife's golden one, and as that limb was in her own control, it was but a doubtful security. The Countess had made a will in which the leg was left to the Count, but life is uncertain—

116

the Countess might outlive her husband; moreover, he was so placed that delay was not only dangerous, but inconvenient. The chronicler thus continues:

"Now, the precious leg while cash was flush,
  Or the Count's acceptance worth a rush,
    Had never excited dissension;
  But no sooner the stocks began to fall,
  Than, without any ossification at all,
  The limb became what people call
    A perfect bone of contention.

"For altered days made altered ways,
  And instead of the complimentary phrase
    So current before her bridal,
  The Countess heard, in language low,
  That her precious leg was precious slow,
  A good 'un to look at, but bad to go,
    And kept quite a sum lying idle.

*   *   *   *   *

"But spite of hint, and threat, and scoff,
    The leg kept its situation;
  For legs are not to be taken off
    By a verbal amputation.

"Firmly then—and more firmly yet—
  With scorn for scorn, and with threat for threat,
    The proud one confronted the cruel;
  And loud and bitter the quarrel arose,
  Fierce and merciless—one of those
  With spoken daggers, and looks like blows—
    In all but the bloodshed a duel.

"Rash and wild, and wretched and wrong,
  Were the words that came from weak and strong,
    Till, maddened for desperate matters,
  Fierce as a tigress escaped from her den,
  She flew to her desk—'twas opened—and then,
  In the time it takes to try a pen,
  Or the clerk to utter his slow 'Amen,'
    Her will was in fifty tatters!

"But the Count, instead of curses wild,
  Only nodded his head and smiled,

As if at the spleen of an angry child;
     But the calm was deceitful and sinister!
And a lull like the lull of the treacherous sea—
For Hate in that moment had sworn to be
The golden leg's sole legatee,
     And that very night to administer."

"THE TORN WILL."

"That very night!"—one more night of golden dreaming, in the midst of which comes death; the deliverer from an existence which the worship of gold has made so pitiful:

"'Tis a stern and startling thing to think,
  How often mortality stands on the brink
     Of its grave without any misgiving:
And yet in this slippery world of strife,
In the stir of human bustle so rife,
There are daily sounds to tell us that life
     Is dying, and Death is living!

"But breath and bloom set doom at nought—

How little the wretched Countess thought,
    When at night she unloosed her sandal,
That the fates had woven her burial-cloth,
And that Death, in the shape of a death's head moth,
    Was fluttering round her candle!

"As she looked at her clock of ormolu,
    For the hours she had gone so wearily through
        At the end of a day of trial,
How little she saw in the pride of prime
The dart of Death in the hand of Time—
    That hand which moved the dial!

"As she went with her taper up the stair,
    How little her swollen eye was aware
        That the shadow which followed was double!
Or when she closed her chamber-door,
    It was shutting out, and for evermore,
        The world and its worldly trouble.

"Little she dreamt as she laid aside
    Her jewels—after one glance of pride—
        They were solemn bequests to Vanity;
Or when her robes she began to doff,
That she stood so near to the putting off
    Of the flesh that clothes humanity.

"And when she quenched the taper's light,
    How little she thought, as the smoke took flight,
That her day was done and merged in a night
    Of dreams and duration uncertain;
        Or along with her own
        That a hand of bone
    Was closing mortality's curtain!

*   *   *   *   *

"Thus, even thus, the Countess slept,
    While death still nearer and nearer crept,
        Like the Thane who smote the sleeping;
But her mind was busy with early joys,
Her golden treasures and golden toys,
        That flashed a bright
        And golden light
    Under lids still red with weeping.

"The golden guineas in silken purse,
  And the 'Golden Legends' she heard from her nurse,
    Of the Mayor in his gilded carriage—
  And London streets that were paved with gold,
  And the golden eggs that were laid of old—
      With each golden thing
      To the golden ring
    At her own auriferous marriage!

"And still the golden light of the sun
  Through her golden dream appeared to run,
  Though the night that roared without was one
    To terrify seamen or gipsies—
  While the moon, as if in malicious mirth,
  Kept peeping down at the ruffled earth,
  As though she enjoyed the tempest's birth,
    In revenge of her old eclipses.

"But vainly, vainly the thunder fell,
  For the soul of the sleeper was under a spell,
    That time had lately embittered—
  The Count, as once at her foot he knelt—
  That foot which now he wanted to melt!
  But, hush! 'twas a stir at her pillow she felt,
    And some object before her glittered.

"'Twas the golden leg! she knew its gleam!
  And up she started and tried to scream;
    But even in the moment she started,
  Down came the limb with a frightful smash,
  And, lost in the universal flash
  That her eyeballs made at so mortal a crash,
    The spark called vital departed.

"Gold, still gold, hard, yellow, and cold,
  For gold she had lived, and died for gold—
    By a golden weapon, not oaken;
  In the morning they found her all alone—
  Stiff, and bloody, and cold as a stone—
  But her leg, the golden leg, was gone,
    And the 'golden bowl was broken.'

"Her Moral.

"Gold! gold! gold! gold!

120

Bright and yellow, hard and cold,
Molten, graven, hammered, and rolled;
Heavy to get, and light to hold;
Hoarded, bartered, bought, and sold,
Stolen, borrowed, squandered, doled;
Spurned by the young, but hugged by the old
To the very verge of the churchyard mould;
Price of many a crime untold;
Gold! gold! gold! gold!
Good or bad a thousandfold!
    How widely its agencies vary—
To save, to ruin, to curse, to bless—
As even its minted coins express,
Now stamped with the image of good Queen Bess,
    And now of Bloody Mary!"

"BEDTIME."

The admirable design—the "tailpiece" to the legend of "Miss Kilmansegg and her Golden Leg"—which Leech calls "Bedtime," is reproduced, not only for its excellence as a composition, but also in evidence of the readiness of the artist's imagination to adopt an idea that has been suggested by the poem, and of the skill with which that cunning hand has realized it. The little old miser has been "counting out his money" with the delight that "time cannot wither, nor custom stale." His shrunken shanks, thin face and hands, betray his age. Death cannot be far off; but no thought apart from the treasure can be spared for the inevitable visitor who surprises the miser at last in the midst of his golden worship. He is far from being tired; but he must go to bed, and sleep the sleep that knows no waking. His skeleton nurse has come for him; her bony hands encircle him. His shroud is on her arm; she cannot wait—no, not for him to handle once more those glittering coins, on which his eye sparkles, and his claw-like fingers make vain attempts to reach.

CHAPTER XX.

DR. JOHN BROWN AND LEECH.

Whether that charming writer, Dr. John Brown, knew Leech in the flesh or not, I cannot say; but that he knew and fully appreciated him in spirit is evident enough in a paper published in a collection of essays entitled "Horæ Subsecivæ." I gather from the concluding passages of the Doctor's brilliant essay that it had been his intention to have written Leech's life, having collected much material for the purpose, but that "ill-health put a stop to this congenial labour." How admirably the labour would have been executed may be shown by the following extracts:

"Leech," says Dr. Brown, "was singularly modest, both as a man and an artist. This came by nature, and was indicative of the harmony and sweetness of his essence; but doubtless the perpetual going to Nature, and drawing out of her fulness, kept him humble, as well as made him rich—made him (what every man of sense and power must be) conscious of his own strength. But before 'the great mother' he was simple and loving, attentive to her lessons as a child, for ever learning and doing."

Again: "Of all our satirists, none have such a pervading sense and power of girlish, ripe, and womanly beauty as Leech…. There is a genuine domesticity about his scenes that could come only from a man who was much at his own fireside, and in the nursery when baby was washed. You see, he is himself *pater familias*, with no Bohemian trait or raffish turn. What he draws, he has seen; what he asks you to live in, and laugh at and with, he has laughed at and lived in. It is this wholesomeness and (to use the right word) this goodness that makes Leech more than a drawer of funny pictures, more even than a great artist. It makes him a teacher and an example of virtue in its widest sense, from that of manliness to the sweet devotion of a woman, and the loving open mouth and eyes of *parvula* on your knee."

I find it difficult to believe that these remarks were written by one who had no personal knowledge of Leech; indeed, I should have thought the writer must have enjoyed an amount of intimacy with him. If Dr. Brown and Leech were strangers to each other, the writer's accurate estimate of the artist shows how exactly the drawings reflect the delightful nature of their producer, so familiar to his nearest friends.

"What we owe to him," adds Dr. Brown, "of wholesome, hearty mirth and pleasure, and of something better than either—good as they are—purity, affection, pluck, humour, kindliness, good-humour, good-feeling, good-breeding, the love of Nature, of one another, of truth, the joys of children, the loveliness of our homely English fields, with their sunsets and village spires, their glimpses into the pure infinite beyond, the sea and all its fulness, its waves 'curling their monstrous heads and hanging them,' their crisping smiles on sunlit sands—all that variety of Nature and of man, which is only less infinite than its Maker! Something of this and of that mysterious quality called humour, that fragrance and flavour of the soul, which God has given us to cheer our lot, to help us to 'take heart and hope and steer right onward,' to have our joke, that lets us laugh and make game of ourselves when we have little else to laugh at or play with, of that which gives us when we will the silver lining of the cloud, and paints a rainbow on the darkened sky out of our own 'troublous tears'—something of all these has this great, simple-hearted, hard-working artist given to us and to our children as a joy and a possession for ever. Let us be grateful to him; let us give him our best honour, affection, and regard."

Walking with Leech one day, we met an old gentleman, to whom I introduced my friend: early in the fifties it was. The old man, though well stricken in years, sported a dark and heavy moustache.

"And so," said Leech, when, after a few commonplaces, we separated, "that is old Mr. Blank the portrait-painter, is it? What on earth induces him to wear purple moustachios?" Purple they were, certainly, and of rather a bright tinge.

"Well," I replied, "he has dyed them, for they were white the other day."

"In my opinion," said Leech, "only soldiers should be allowed moustachios."

In my early days, that "hirsute appendage" created such a prejudice against the wearers as would not be credited in these beard-bearing times. There were places of business the doors of which were closed against the moustache. At a well-known bank complete shaving of moustache and beard is insisted upon to this day. The sufferings of our troops in the Crimea were sufficiently agonizing without the torment or even the possibility of the morning's shave; and it is to the Russian campaign we owe the "beard movement," which from that time to the present is so universal. Our officers returned from their battles covered with glory and hair, and so much improved by the latter—in the opinion of those whose approval was most valued—as to make a sacrifice of it out of the question. Little did Leech imagine when he made his sweeping objection to the moustache, what a factor he would find it in his future work. How many delightful sketches turn upon it! Who can forget those two little rival snobs—rivals in the love of some fair approver of beards—who have withdrawn themselves from society during the incubation of their moustachios, and who, having accidentally sought the same suburban retirement, meet face to face, stubbly beard to stubbly beard, at a corner of a lane? And that precocious young gentleman who asks his sisters if they approve of the removal of a moustache, the presence of which they had never been able to discover!

Under the heading of "The Beard Movement," we have a British swell in a fainting state in the arms of a policeman; this serious condition having arisen from the sight of a postman with moustachios. In another drawing, policemen are marching to their posts of duty decorated by beards of such magnitude as to strike terror into the street boys, who scatter in all directions at the sight of them.

In "Pictures of Life and Character" other examples of the alarm excited by the beard movement are given with the refined humour peculiar to Leech.

I find I have to modify somewhat my conviction that Leech rarely adopted the subjects proposed to him for illustration; no doubt by far the largest number were the outcome of his own conception, or observation of incidents in his experience; but I have proof of several examples to the contrary. For instance, Mr. Holman Hunt says: "One Friday night I had sat down to much correspondence, intending before concluding to write of two or three amusing facts picked up that might suit him (Leech) for illustration. It had become very late, and I was clearing away my paper, when, with vexation, I remembered his letter had not been written. I seized the pen, and on a page I drew two horizontal lines quite dividing the space. In the top I put: 'Scene— Kitchen garden, country cottage. *Dramatis Personæ*: Factotum, master entering,' and then a line or two of dialogue.

"The second subject I treated similarly, and the third also, which was not so promising. I enclosed this without a word to Leech, and posted it with my other letters about two in the morning. The following Wednesday the two subjects, admirably treated, were in *Punch*. When next I saw him he was eager with excuses for not having written. He added: 'The letter when it was opened at breakfast was most opportune, for I had to leave town by five, and I was bound to furnish two designs before going, and I had come down without having the wildest notion what to do. The subjects in your note were ready-made, and I was able to sketch them without a moment's waste of time.'"

Mr. Hunt tells an anecdote of Kenny Meadows, the jovial Bohemian, whom, I hope, the reader of these pages may remember, that is so characteristic and amusing, and illustrative of his own nature and of that of Leech, that I insert it in this place. "Meadows was quite at the head of the *Punch* artists when Leech joined them, and was naturally delighted by the praise bestowed upon his drawings by 'this ruler amongst the illustrators of *Punch*.' He—Meadows —declared that a sight of Leech's illustrations had so disgusted him with his own work that he felt inclined to give up art altogether. 'Why,' said he, 'should I go on giving proof after proof of my incapacity when you leave me so far behind?' This modest effusion was uttered early in the evening, and before the setting in of the gin-and-water period, which was destined to effect a striking change in Meadows' estimate of himself, and of the recent addition to the pictorial staff.

"Leech was a sincere admirer of Meadows' work, and of this he assured the self-condemning artist in no measured terms, instancing for special praise many of Kenny's designs brimming over with poetic conceits in the illustrations of Shakespeare. Meadows listened to Leech's compliments, and said it was 'deuced liberal' of him to say what he did. He then mixed himself a glass of gin and water, saying, 'Well, after all, it's wise to make the best of things, and be as jolly as one can under all circumstances.'

"The two artists then fell into general conversation, and into—on the part of one of them—the imbibing of much gin and water. Under the influence of the latter, Meadows returned to the subject of his own works, and proceeded to show in what respect they surpassed those of others—even Leech's, which were worthless from the absence of 'poetry,' which ought to sanctify all art.

"'Give me imagination or nothing, my dear boy!' he exclaimed. 'I don't want your commonplace facts done with a little trick of caricature, as it is called. Why don't you aim at something better, something higher? I would rather do nothing than the things you do, which, not only in design, but in execution, are unworthy of a true artist.'"

All this was told to my friend by Leech himself, and, says Mr. Hunt, "Leech's shrug of the shoulders, expressive of bearing infinite disgrace, was the gesture of a comedian, but a hearty, good-natured laugh gave the real expression of the feeling left in his kind soul; there was not a jot of malice there against the severe judgment upon himself. The Scandinavian hero returning so sedate from victory that he might have been supposed to have suffered a defeat, or from disaster in the field, so composed that he might have been thought victorious, could not have surpassed Leech's manner in accepting both the praise and the censure of his elder rival."

Another old friend of mine, Mr. Horsley, R.A., offers further proof of Leech's occasional acceptance of suggestions for his designs. In the course of a walk Mr. Horsley was accosted by one of those itinerant traders to whom the street is the shop, and solicited to buy a rope of onions.

"Take the last rope, sir," says the man. My friend looks like a prosperous gentleman, to whom the offer might be made with a prospect of success, though the awkwardness of his appearance with the addition of a long rope of large onions in his hand would most likely prove a deterrent to the purchase. Mr. Horsley declined the offer, but it instantly occurred to him that such a proposal, if made to one of Leech's "swells," would be intensely comic, and he accordingly mentioned the incident to Leech, who smiled as usual and said nothing. A drawing, however, appeared immediately in *Punch*, but, strange to say, the incident is defrauded of much, if not all, its humour. The swell leaves nothing to be desired, except that he certainly should have been alone, and not, as according to Leech, accompanied by a lady, to whom the onions might have been useful. The absurdity surely consisted in the ludicrous position of a young gentleman who was subjected to an offer of which he would scarcely know the meaning, and much less likely to take advantage of it. My friend expressed his disappointment to Leech, who, with characteristic modesty, acknowledged his mistake.

"I may mention another curious failure," says Mr. Horsley. "Leech came into my room one day roaring with laughter at a story he had just heard of two small boys who had been overheard discussing the age of a companion, and one said to the other, 'Well, I don't 'zactly know how old Charley is; but he must be very old, for he blows his own nose.' This is delightful as coming from the little chaps that Leech drew so perfectly; but, wonderful to relate, he represented the conversation as passing between a boy looking fourteen or fifteen and a girl in a riding-habit."

"He Blows His Nose."

I subjoin the first idea of that which seems to be the incident told to Mr. Horsley, though it fails to illustrate the scene as described by Mr. Horsley, or the rendering of it afterwards adopted by Leech. The sketch, however, will show the rough manner in which all the thoughts so perfectly expressed on the wood-block were first sketched by the artist.

CHAPTER XXI.

AUTOGRAPH-HUNTERS AND OTHERS.

No doubt all painters, poets, literary men, Churchmen—in short, all men who have attained to more or less celebrity—become the prey of the autograph-hunter, either in the form of a boy at school, a young lady whose life is made continuous sunshine by the contemplation of your pictures or the study of your delightful poems, or an elderly gentleman who has watched your career with intense interest from its beginning. Each of these applicants, strange to say, avers that he or she will be made happier by the possession of your name on a card or a piece of paper which is enclosed for your signature, and in addition to your "valued name," if you happen to be an artist, "if you will add a slight sketch," the gratitude of the hunter will know no bounds. I have been guilty on one or two occasions of complying with a desire that seems to verge upon the unreasonable; but my folly is as nothing compared to that of Edwin Landseer, who was a frequent and willing victim to such imposition. On one of the many occasions when I had the happiness of receiving Landseer at my house, the conversation turned upon the autograph-hunter, whose habits were strongly anathematized by some of us; the great painter defended the craze as harmless, easily gratified, and complimentary to the objects of it.

"Only this morning," said he, "I had an application from someone at Birmingham for my name, and for a sketch of a dog's head added to it; well, I complied with both desires."

I confess to my surprise when I heard this, and I was amused on hearing artists who were present exclaim loudly against such a proceeding, as creating a precedent that they would be expected to follow. Harmless, however, is the autograph pest in comparison with the really terrible *album*, which bids unblushingly for work that may consume many hours of the time of the painter or the poet. Here, again, Landseer was a great sinner; many a splendidly bound album lies at this moment on gilded tables in stately English mansions, the homes of our "old nobility," with delightful drawings of sporting scenes by that cunning hand; and there are instances, I am sorry to say, of the possessors being unable to resist the sums offered for the purchase of their treasures so cheaply acquired.

As I am speaking of Edwin Landseer, I seize the opportunity of expressing my great regret that my friend Mr. Sidney Cooper, R.A., in his recently published memoirs, should have created an impression in the public mind that Landseer was a drunkard. From my intimate knowledge of Landseer, I can aver that nothing could be further from the fact. I have dined in his company scores of times, and I have met him in all kinds of society, and under conditions which would have made the propensity, if it possessed him, irresistible; and never in a single instance did I, or anyone else, see Landseer even *excited* by drink. This was the habit of the man until about a year and a half before his death, when the brain disorder began which afterwards destroyed him. I cannot disguise from myself that if Mr. Cooper had questioned the physicians who attended Landseer in his last illness, he would have been told that a craving for drink of every kind is one of the peculiarities of the disease which every sufferer from it is quite unable to resist. I know that great care was taken to keep stimulants from the illustrious patient; but that he may have secretly possessed himself of wine or spirits on certain occasions, and in that way given a colour to the report of his drunken habits, is probable enough; but I venture to think a brother-artist—even if the charge of habitual intoxication could have been proved against this great painter—should have been mournfully silent; how much more careful, then, should he have been, if he desired—perhaps as a warning—to proclaim this terrible failing, to ascertain whether he had truthful ground to go upon.

I do not in the least apologize for the above, though it is "far wide" of the purpose of this chapter; but I feel that my complaint against albums is a little ungracious and ungrateful in the face of the admirable page of sketches with which my publisher has supplied me. (See note at the end of this chapter.)

Mr. Richard Bentley was the possessor of an autograph-book and album combined; but he did not solicit the aid of strangers to fill it, thereby creating a wide difference between himself and the ordinary album nuisance. "My father," says Mr. George Bentley, "started an autograph-book, and got Cruikshank, Leech, and some others to give a sketch, or, if not an artist, an autograph. Leech did one in colour. It was so superior to anything in the volume that I cut it out and framed it, and so see it every day in my life."

The idea is to reproduce some of the characters he was so fond of sketching, and some he had actually given; for instance, the girl in bed is, I think, from the scene where a man gets up at night to fire at some cats. The wife suddenly awakes, and finds him looking out of window, gun in hand, and imagines

thieves. The *voyez vous* 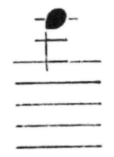 is delicious,

and the old gentleman with "Now, it's my opinion," etc., I am pretty sure is taken from a sketch in some work he had illustrated.

So far Mr. George Bentley, who shows that his father, who was the liberal employer of Leech, Dickens, Cruikshank, and so many others, had a *raison d'être* for his requests in favour of his album.

I supplement Mr. Bentley's remarks on this delightful page by calling my readers' special attention to that charming little boy and his dreadful old grandmother—"Will Charley come and live with his gran-ma?" Study well that little boy's face, beautiful as an angel's, as he looks wondering at the hideous old woman—will he live with her? not, I think, if he can help it. See, also, the lovely little group of the ill-assorted couple—old husband and young wife. More terrible the lady's fate there than Charley's with his "Gran-ma."

I have now to notice another album belonging to no less a person than the late Duke of Devonshire. Leech made the Duke's acquaintance while staying with Millais at the Peacock, Baslow, a place within easy distance of Chatsworth; where, by the way, Millais painted the perfect likeness of Leech which, by his kindness, is allowed to enrich this volume, and where, by Sir Joseph Paxton, I think, Leech was introduced to the Duke, and entertained with much kindness at Chatsworth. How the album was introduced to Leech, and whether the Duke asked for a sketch or the artist volunteered it, I have no evidence to offer; but that a design was made and repeated, the following letters from the Duke sufficiently prove:

"August 6, 1851.

"Dear Sir,

"I am so much charmed with your device that I must have a seal engraved from it. Perhaps you would have the kindness to renew the sketch for me on a smaller scale, as I am unwilling to extract the leaf made valuable by you from the book. The stone should not be larger than this, which, I fear, makes my request hardly possible.

"Most sincerely yours,
"DEVONSHIRE."

The Seal.

The reduced scale proved no obstacle, and the success was gracefully acknowledged as follows:

"London, April 14, 1852.

"Dear Sir,

"In these critical days of the Crystal Palace, let me request your acceptance of the seal for which you gave me the idea.

"And that you may not have any feeling as to depriving me of it, I must tell you that I have another.

"Believe me,
"Most sincerely yours,
"Devonshire."

But what was the subject of the drawing? In a courteous reply to my inquiry, I find from the present Duke that he has no such drawing in any of his books, and he knows nothing of the seal. In a postscript to one of Leech's letters to his friend Adams, however, I find the following mention of it:

"Look at the seal on this envelope. I told you, I think, some time ago about my making a little sketch for the Duke of Devonshire, and how kind he was about it, saying he must have a seal made of it. Well, he called here himself, and left me a most handsome and valuable seal the other day, of which, I confess, I am proud to send you an impression. As you say of some of your people, 'It's very nice to be treated so, isn't it?' The design of the seal is a spade turning up the Crystal Palace, in allusion to Paxton being a gardener.

"Ever yours, my dear Charley,

"John Leech.

"31, Notting Hill Terrace,
"April 20, 1852."

Though the present Duke of Devonshire knows nothing of the seal, or the drawing from which it was made, I am happy to say that I am able to present to my readers an impression from it, through the kindness of Leech's son-in-law, Mr. Gillett, to whom I applied in my perplexity.

Everybody may not know that Sir Joseph Paxton, the Duke of Devonshire's gardener, was the architect of the glass house of 1851, afterwards christened the Crystal Palace, which—greatly enlarged—now flourishes at Sydenham. I conclude this chapter with an extract from *Notes and Queries*, evidently written by a friend of Leech. The writer, under date November, 1864, says:

"Leech's success was owing to his almost daily practice of jotting in his note-book every remarkable physiognomy or incident that struck him in his rambles. Such, at any rate, was his practice at the commencement of his too brief career. On one occasion he and I were riding to town together in an omnibus, when an elderly gentleman in a very peculiar dress, and with very marked features, stepped into the vehicle, and sat down immediately in front of us. We were the only inside passengers. For whom or for what he took, or probably mistook, us, I know not; but he stared so hard, and made such wry faces at us, that I could hardly refrain from laughter. My discomfiture was almost completed when Leech suddenly exclaimed, 'By the way, did Prendergast ever show you that extraordinary account that has been recently forwarded to him?' and, showing me his note-book, added, 'Just run your eye up that column, and tell me what you can make of it.' Instead of a column, the features of the old gentleman were reflected upon the page with life-like fidelity. On another occasion I saw him strike off with promptitude and skill the scene of a quarrel between some dirty little urchins in a suburban village."

Note.—To my great regret, I find that the material in which Mr. Bentley's drawing was executed made its reproduction impossible.

CHAPTER XXII.

ARTISTS' LIVES.

"Silent, gentle, forbearing, his indignation flashed forth an eloquence when roused by anything mean or ungenerous. Manly in all his thoughts, tastes, and habits, there was about him an almost feminine tenderness. He would sit by the bedside, and smooth the pillow of a sick child with the gentleness of a woman. No wonder he was the idol of those around him, but it is the happiness of such a life that there is so little to be told of it."

I do not know to what friend of Leech's we are indebted for these few words; which are, however, sufficient to convey a perfect idea of the subject of them to those to whom he was only known by his works.

The lives of most artists are uneventful. Leech's short life was especially so. His incessant labour prevented his giving the time to what is called society— that is so often devoted to it—to the loss of the happiness that home always afforded to him. He was a self-sacrificing and most dutiful son, a good and loving father and husband, and a true and faithful friend. In the quotation above we read that there is little to be told of Leech's life. I have talked with those who had the happiness of greater intimacy with him than I can boast of, without being able to learn anything beyond the ordinary events of an everyday life, void of dramatic incident, commonplace in fact, except for the constant triumph of an unapproachable genius.

Leech had a large circle of friends and acquaintances, with here and there an aristocrat amongst the latter; but his intimates were few: between them and him, however, there were unusually strong ties of affectionate regard; his nervous, modest, retiring nature often conveyed a false impression of him to casual acquaintances. I have heard him described as haughty, "stand-offish," cold, and so on; and his manner to some of those who may have met him for the first time, occasionally admitted of that construction; but it arose from nervousness, or from an aversion to loud and ill-timed compliment, feeling, as he sincerely did, his "little sketches" deserved no such eulogium. Though Leech's life offers no field for the description of stirring events, the delightful nature of the man affords matchless opportunities for study, reflection, and emulation; and that study may be pursued in the examination of his works, in which, as in a looking-glass, the nature of their producer is reflected. There may be seen ever-recurring proofs of the artist's intense love of Nature in all her forms; whether he deals with woman, the most beautiful of all Nature's works, or with children in the endless variety of their attractiveness, absolute truth, tenderness and beauty are paramount; and not only are these creatures natural and beautiful, but the artist is at one with them in all their doings, from the sympathy peculiar to him with all that is simple, pure, and lovable. Side by side with this tenderness of heart, we have a robust manliness which shows itself constantly.

As a matter of course Leech's love of Nature was not confined to humanity, but was extended to the animal creation, to the trees and the fields, the sea-shore and the sea—in short, to every form of animate and inanimate nature. Think what a delight such a constituted heart and mind must be to the possessor of them! and not only to him, but to us to whom he so freely offers the results of his sympathies, making us certainly happier, and it is to be hoped better, by the taking in of so much that is exhilarating, healthy, and true. Evidence is frequent of pity for the sufferings of the poor and the oppressed. In many a scene Leech becomes a warm sympathizer with unmerited distress; and constantly his honest heart is stirred into indignation at some instance of injustice; then we find that the pencil which can deal so gently with childhood and woman can also, in indelible lines, stigmatize the stony-hearted oppressor.

Underlying the refined and delicate humour that distinguishes the greater part of Leech's work we frequently find some more or less serious social grievance smartly satirized. In "Servant-Gal-ism," for example, the airs and graces, the impudent assumption, and the dishonesty even, which sometimes disgrace those otherwise worthy people, are shown to us in drawings so humorous as to make us laugh heartily, but at the same time we feel the full force of the satire intended. In the encounters between servant-girls and their mistresses the ladies sometimes get the worst of it; notably in a drawing that represents a mistress and her maid in conflict respecting the dressing of their hair. The old lady has tortured her few remaining locks into miserable little ringlets, that make a shocking contrast to the long curls of her young and pretty servant; and no sooner does she catch sight of the girl's ringlets, than she angrily tells her she will not permit such bare-faced imitation of the way she chooses to wear her hair. Here I am afraid we cannot help feeling a certain amount of contempt for the blind vanity and tyranny of the mistress, while we sympathize with the maid.

Footmen afford a wide field for the good-humoured banter of Leech.

Amongst the many striking proofs of the genius that distinguished him, is one that to me, as an artist, is astonishing. I allude to the individual character with which Leech invests each of his servant-girls and footmen, as well as every type that comes under his hand. I have not counted the number of servants of "all sorts and sizes" that appear in "Pictures of Life and Character," but I am quite sure that a comparison of one with another will prove that not one can be found in the slightest degree to resemble another; each is an individual by himself or herself, separate and distinct—a footman from top to toe; take away his uniform, and, from some peculiarity of manner or action, he is unmistakably a footman still. The same may be said of the maid-servants, in whom Leech's wonderful power of individualizing is shown even more palpably; for the cook is a cook, and perfectly distinct from the scullery-maid and the charwoman; and no two cooks or kitchen-maids resemble each other personally, but only in their offices.

The same may be truly said of numberless types immortalized by Leech; but, strange to say, it cannot be said of the *young* ladies: they almost all have a family likeness to one another—a resemblance that can be traced to Mrs. Leech. This fault, for it is a fault, and a grave one, is as strange to me as the infinite variety shown in his representation of all sorts and conditions of men and women is astounding. In marking this I point to the only shortcoming in all Leech's work, and though, as I think (I may be wrong), he has this fault in his treatment of young ladies, it is absent in his drawings of elderly or old ones; the aristocratic or plebeian old women are as well marked in personal contrast with each other as the rest of his delightful creations.

The rest of his creations! What a dazzling, bewildering mass of humanity crowds upon the mind when one attempts to point out special scenes for examination and criticism! If I were to say a tithe of what I feel about hundreds of Leech's drawings, I should greatly exceed the space permitted to me in this book, and I should also show how inferior my powers of analysis are to those of Dickens and Thackeray, and others whose delightful appreciation of beauty, humour and character are so eloquently set forth elsewhere in this memoir; and perhaps I may add that I have sufficient respect for the intelligence of my readers to convince me that they require no directions from me as to when they should laugh and when look grave, or where to discover the point of a joke that is palpable to the "meanest capacity."

With Leech's work in an artistic sense I have more to do. Considering the limited means employed, the results produced are very wonderful. Nothing is left to desire in character or expression; the story is perfectly told in every drawing; and it can be read without reference to the few lines beneath, which in the wording of them appear to me as perfect as the cuts themselves. The composition of groups and figures, which looks so simple and natural, is the result of consummate art. The drawing, notably of figures and animals in action, is always correct. Chiaroscuro is too comprehensive a word to apply to the light and shadow of Leech's drawings; but in what we call "black and white," or, in other words, in the distribution of the masses of dark, and what I may term semi-dark, and light, they are always skilfully effective.

I have been told that Leech's work, in the opinion of a high authority in matters of art, resembles, and successfully rivals, the silver-point drawings of the old masters. I have seen many examples of those beautiful drawings, but I have never seen one that bore the faintest resemblance to the way in which Leech "lays his lines." The same judge tells us that Leech's work betrays an ignorance of the principles of effect—in other words, a neglect of the laws that should guide an artist in the selection of his scheme of light and shadow. An intelligent glance at any of Leech's drawings will show the fallibility of that judgment.

CHAPTER XXIII.

LEECH EXHIBITION.

About the year 1860—or thereabouts—there was exhibited in London a huge picture of Nero contemplating the ruins of Rome, by a German artist named Piloti. On seeing the picture I was much struck by a certain somewhat coarse vigour in the work, which asserted itself in spite of crude and harsh colouring; the principal figure—as often happens—was disappointing and theatrical. Nero stood in a melodramatic posture, with his arms folded, enjoying the destruction of the city. Leech, accompanied by his friend, the late Sir Edgar Boehm, R.A. (the eminent sculptor who made an admirable statuette of Leech), saw the picture, and after a long study of it he turned to Boehm and said: "I would rather have been the painter of that picture than the producer of all the things I have ever perpetrated!" Leech's friend received this avowal with incredulous laughter, and, pointing out some of the glaring faults of the Nero, endeavoured to convince his companion that one of his drawings was worth acres of such work as Piloti's; in which I, for one, entirely agree with him.

The hankering after oil-colours which always possessed Leech was destined to be gratified; for soon after this—in 1862—he came before the public as the painter of a series of "sketches in oil," being reproductions of his own drawings in *Punch*. These—almost virgin—attempts were exhibited at the Egyptian Hall, where they were visited by thousands of admiring spectators, who left several thousand pounds behind them. Everyone knows what a few inches of space are taken up by one of Leech's drawings as it appears in "Pictures of Life and Character." A sketch of such small dimensions would have been ineffective in colours, and it was owing to an invention by which the originals were enlarged, that the artist was enabled to offer to the public copies of drawings four or five inches square, increased in some instances to three feet by two.

"'The idea originated,' says Dr. Brown, 'with Mr. Mark Lemon, Leech's friend and colleague, who saw that by a new invention—a beautiful piece of machinery—the impression of a block in *Punch* being first taken on a sheet of indiarubber, was enlarged; when by a lithographic process the copy thus got could be transferred to the stone and impressions printed upon a large sheet of canvas. Having thus obtained an outline groundwork, consisting of his own lines enlarged to some eight times the area of the original block, Leech proceeded to colour these. His knowledge of the manipulation of oil-colours was very slight, and it was under the guidance of his friend Millais that his first attempts were made, and crude enough they were. He used a kind of transparent colour, which allowed the coarse lines of the enlargement to show through, so that the production presented the appearance of indifferent lithographs slightly tinted. In a short time he obtained great mastery over oil-colour, and instead of allowing the thick, fatty lines of printer's ink to remain on the canvas, he, by the use of turpentine, removed the ink, particularly with regard to the lines of the faces and figures. These he redrew with his own hand in a fine and delicate manner. To this he added a delicacy of finish, particularly in flesh-colour, which greatly enhanced the value and beauty of his later works."

The catalogue to the sketches in oil is prefaced by a few modest words by the artist, who concludes some remarks upon their production thus:

"These sketches have no claim to be regarded, or tested, as finished pictures. It is impossible for anyone to know the fact better than I do. They have no pretensions to a higher name than the name I give them, 'Sketches in Oil.'"

The exhibition consisted of sixty-seven works, and the room containing them was filled all day long by a laughing crowd. Leech shrank from crowds at all times, and an assembly drawn together by his own works would have special terrors for him. After the opening of the gallery he was never known to visit it, mainly from his innate modesty, but also from his dread of being "caught and talked at by enthusiastic people."

A story is told of a visit of a sporting lord who took his huntsman—whose judgment of hounds and horses was celebrated for its acumen—to give his verdict on the Leech Exhibition in general, and on dogs and horses in particular.

"'Ah, my lord, nothin' but a party as knows 'osses could have drawed them there 'unters.'"

If the huntsman offered an opinion on other features of the exhibition, it is not recorded; he criticised only what he understood—therein giving a much-needed example to many critics.

In the few remarks in the way of criticism on the Leech Exhibition which I allow myself to make, I claim to be in the position of the huntsman whose experience of the horse made his opinion of that animal valuable; my own experience of pictures, as it extends over fifty years, may fairly claim for me the right of judgment, and I acknowledge myself to be one of those who thought the exhibition of "Sketches in Oil" did not increase Leech's reputation; though it happily did increase his own fortune, or the fortune of somebody else.

Dr. Brown says that Leech "obtained a great mastery over oil-colours." The huntsman may have thought as much; if he did, he was as much in error as Dr. Brown. The sketches lost much charm by their enlargement, and they were further greatly damaged by the crude and inharmonious way in which they were coloured. The girls' lovely faces, which delight us so thoroughly in their pencilled forms, became almost vulgar under the artist's attempts to paint flesh—the most difficult of all things to render truly. When he first gives them to us fresh from the wood block, conveying to us, as he does, the most ravishing beauty by a few pencil-marks, we paint the faces for ourselves with the colours and brushes of the mind, with a result unattainable by the colourman's tools unless they are in the hands of a Reynolds or a Vandyke. Leech's delightful backgrounds, too, were terribly spoilt by his oil-paints: air and distance disappeared altogether in many of them. But it is time my grumbling gave place to what Mr. Thackeray had to say about the Leech Exhibition in the *Times* of June 21, 1862:

"Now, while Mr. Leech has been making his comments upon our society and manners, one of the wittiest and keenest observers has been giving a description of his own country of France in a thousand brilliant pages; and it is a task not a little amusing and curious for a student of manners to note the difference between the two satirists—perhaps between the societies they describe. Leech's England is a country peopled by noble elderly squires, riding large-boned horses, followed across country by lovely beings of the most gorgeous proportions, by respectful retainers, by gallant little boys emulating the pluck and courage of the sire. The joke is the precocious courage of the child, his gallantry as he charges his fences, his coolness as he eyes the glass of port, or tells grandpapa he likes his champagne dry. How does Gavarni represent the family father, the sire, the old gentleman, in *his* country—the civilized country? Paterfamilias, in a dyed wig and whiskers, is leaning by the side of Mademoiselle Coralie on her sofa in the Rue de Bréda. Paterfamilias, with a mask and a nose half a yard long, is hobbling after her at the ball. The *enfant terrible* is making papa and mamma alike ridiculous by showing us mamma's lover, who is lurking behind the screen. A thousand volumes are written protesting against the seventh commandment. The old man is for ever hunting after the young woman; the wife is for ever cheating the husband. The fun of the old comedy never seems to end in France, and we have the word of their own satirists, novelists, painters of society, that it is being played from day to day.

"In the works of that barbarian artist, Hogarth, the subject which affords such playful sport to the civilized Frenchman is stigmatized as a fearful crime, and is visited by a ghastly retribution. The English savage never thinks of such a crime as funny, and, a hundred years after Hogarth, our modern 'painter of mankind' still retains his barbarous modesty, is tender with children, decorous before women, has never once thought he had the right or calling to wound the modesty of either.

"Mr. Leech surveys society from the gentleman's point of view. In old days, when Mr. Jerrold lived and wrote for that famous periodical, he took the other side; he looked up at the rich and great with a fierce, a sarcastic aspect, and a threatening posture, and his outcry or challenge was: 'Ye rich and great, look out! We, the people, are as good as you. Have a care, ye priests, wallowing on a tithe pig and rolling in carriages and four; ye landlords, grinding the poor; ye vulgar fine ladies, bullying innocent governesses, and what not—we will expose your vulgarity, we will put down your oppression, we will vindicate the nobility of our common nature,' and so forth. A great deal has to be said on the Jerrold side, a great deal was said, perhaps, even, a great deal too much. It is not a little curious to speculate upon the works of these two famous contributors to *Punch*, these two 'preachers,' as the phrase is. 'Woe to you, you tyrant and heartless oppressor of the poor!' calls out Jerrold as Dives' carriage rolls by. 'Beware of the time when your bloated coachman shall be hurled from his box, when your gilded flunkey shall be cast to the earth from his perch, and your pampered horses shall run away with you and your vulgar wife and smash you into ruin.' The other philosopher looks at Dives and his cavalcade in his own peculiar manner. He admires the horses and copies, with the most curious felicity, their forms and action. The footmen's calves and powder, the coachman's red face and flock wig, the over-dressed lady and plethoric gentleman in the carriage, he depicts with the happiest strokes; and if there is a pretty girl and a rosy child on the back seat, he 'takes them up tenderly' and touches them with a hand that has a caress in it. The artist is very tender to all these little people. It is hard to say whether he loves girls or boys most—those delightful little men on their ponies in the hunting field, those charming little Lady Adas flirting at the juvenile ball, or Tom the butcher's boy on the slide, or ragged little Emily pulling the go-cart, freighted with Elizerann and her doll. Steele, Fielding, Goldsmith, Dickens, are similarly tender in their pictures of children. We may be barbarians, monsieur; but even savages are occasionally kind to their papooses. 'When are the holidays?' Mothers of families ought to come to this exhibition and bring the children. Then there are the full-grown young ladies—the very full-grown young ladies—dancing in the ball-room or reposing by the sea-shore: the men can peep at whole seraglios of these beauties for the moderate charge of one shilling, and bring away their charming likenesses in the illustrated catalogue (two-and-six). In the 'Mermaids' Haunt,' for instance, there is a siren combing her golden locks, and another dark-eyed witch actually sketching you as you look at her, whom Ulysses could not resist. To walk by the side of the much-sounding sea and come upon such a bevy of beauties as this, what bliss for a man or a painter! The mermaids in that haunt, haunt the beholder for hours after. Where is the shore on which those creatures were sketched? The sly catalogue does not tell us.

"The outdoor sketcher will not fail to remark the excellent fidelity with which Mr. Leech draws the backgrounds of his little pictures. The homely landscape, the sea, the winter road by which the huntsmen ride, the light and clouds, the birds floating overhead, are indicated by a few strokes which show the artist's untiring watchfulness and love of Nature. He is a natural truth-teller, as Hogarth was before him, and indulges in no flights of fancy. He speaks his mind out quite honestly like a thorough Briton. He loves horses, dogs, river and field sports. He loves home and children—that you can see. He holds Frenchmen in light esteem. A bloated 'mosoo,' walking Leicester Square with a huge cigar and a little hat, with *billard* and *estaminet* written on his flaccid face, is a favourite study with him; the unshaven jowl, the waist tied with a string, the boots which pad the quadrant pavement—this dingy and disreputable being exercises a fascination over Mr. Punch's favourite artist.

"We trace, too, in his work a prejudice against the Hebrew nation, against the natives of an island much celebrated for its verdure and its wrongs. These are lamentable prejudices indeed, but what man is without his own? No man has ever depicted the little 'snob' with such a delightful touch. Leech fondles and dances this creature as he does the children. To remember one or two of these dear gents is to laugh. To watch them looking at their own portraits in this pleasant gallery will be no small part of the exhibition; and as we can all go and see our neighbours caricatured here, it is just possible that our neighbours may find some smart likenesses of *their* neighbours in these brilliant, life-like, good-natured *Sketches in Oil*."

The publication of this sympathetic article in such a paper as the *Times*, by such a writer as Thackeray, no doubt increased the popularity of "Sketches in Oil." However that may have been, its appearance gave the keenest pleasure to Leech, who is said to have "rejoiced like a child, exclaiming:

"'That's like putting a thousand pounds into my pocket!'"

By far the best examples of Leech's oil paintings are in the collection of his old warmly attached friend, Mr. Charles Adams, of Barkway. Instead of a garish stain of washy colour merely passed over an engraving, these small sporting subjects are painted in a good solid style, well drawn and carefully finished; carrying with them the conviction, to my mind, that Leech might possibly have been as great with the brush as he was with the lead pencil.

Amongst the "Pictures of Life and Character" there is a drawing of two young ladies sitting *vis-à-vis* on a rustic seat; from the books held by both of them it might be supposed they were reading, as no doubt they were, till one of them caught sight of their partners at the ball the night before, who by a strange coincidence are advancing upon them through the wood. The drawing is entitled "Remarkable Occurrence," with the following explanation: "On the morning after the dispensary ball, as Emily Deuxtemps and Clara Polkington were sitting in the plantation, who should come to the very spot but Captain Fastman and young Reginald Phipps!"

I forget the year in which this drawing appeared. The scene is laid at Scarborough, where Leech was passing his summer holiday. I was so taken with the beauty of the girls, the composition of the drawing, and its general adaptability to the making of an oil picture, that I wrote to the artist; and, pointing out these characteristics, begged him to "paint the subject." I received no reply to my entreaty, but on meeting him afterwards in London, he apologized, and declared he would take my advice.

"You don't mind my not answering you, old fellow: I hate letter-writing. It was very kind of you to write—glad you like the girls on the garden-seat. Well, I will try my hand at it the moment *I have time to spare*." The time never came. A "Remarkable Occurrence" did not even appear amongst the "Sketches in Oil."

It would have been a very onerous task for a man in perfect health, and accustomed to the use of the brush, to have prepared those sixty-seven sketches in oil for exhibition, even if his time could have been wholly devoted to it. To Leech, with the hand of Death nearly touching him, in almost entire ignorance of the method in which he was working—the ordeal was terrible. To the entreaties of his friends that he should stick less closely to his easel at Lowestoft or Whitby, he would reply that the fine air of the former, and the picturesque scenery abounding at the latter, were intended for idle people, and not for him.

To the man with well-strung nerves Leech's sensibility to noises of all kinds seems incomprehensible; but for years before the oil sketches were undertaken I knew of his sufferings from himself; and the world must have guessed them from his attacks upon the organ-grinders, the bellowing street-hawkers, and the thousand and one noises that distress the London householder whose livelihood depends upon his brain. Of course most of the drawings in which the organ-grinder and the itinerant vendor of stale fish figure, are highly humorous; causing the unthinking to laugh, unconscious of the terrible seriousness under which they have been produced.

Humour was so much a part of Leech's nature that it sometimes asserted itself incongruously. For example: One evening a convivial party of the Ancient

144

Order of Foresters returning from, perhaps, the Crystal Palace, where high festival had been held, roused poor Leech almost to madness by a yelling uproar opposite his door. He left his work, and rushed bare-headed amongst them.

"What are you making this horrible row for?"

Then seeing the extraordinary Robin Hood kind of costume affected by these people, he said:

"What's it all about—who are you?"

"We are Foresters, that's what we are," was the reply.

"Then, why on earth don't you go into a forest and make your infernal row there, instead of disturbing a whole street with your noise?" said Leech.

There is no doubt that hyper-sensitiveness to noises troubled Leech "from his youth up," for we find in comparatively early drawings in *Punch* examples of the nuisances created by the fish-hawkers, and the sellers of the great variety of things that nobody wants, at the different seaside places where he took his so-called holidays. He was naturally hard upon the encouragers of these pests. There is an inimitable sketch of an old lady who has called an organ-grinder into her parlour. The man, a perfect type of the Italian performer, grinds away at his instrument, the old woman snaps her fingers and kicks up her heels in mad delight; her parrot screams, and her dog howls an accompaniment. Cake and wine are on the table, and there is a stuffed cat in a glass case on the wall. The drawing is called a "Fancy Sketch of the Old Party who rather likes Organ-grinding."

In another sketch an elderly paterfamilias is seen sitting upon the beach attempting to read his newspaper under the difficulties caused by a boy with guinea-pigs, and others with something to sell; a sailor proposes a sail, an old woman has a box of baby linen, and the inevitable sweetstuff merchant looms in the near distance. The drawing is entitled "The Bores of the Beach," with the following explanatory lines:

"So, as it's a fine day, you'll sit on the beach and read the paper comfortably, will you? Very good! Then we recommend you to get what guinea-pigs, brandy-balls, boats, and children's socks, to say nothing of shell-work boxes, lace collars, and the like you may want, before you settle down."

Perhaps the drawing that most happily illustrates the terrible suffering that is caused by those wandering minstrels, the Italian organ-grinders, is in double form—two *scenes*, so to speak. The first represents a dignified, middle-aged father of a family who stands at his door "expostulating with an organ-grinder, who is defying him with extreme insolence, alternated with performances on the instrument of torture," says Leech. The Italian, who is an embodiment of brutal impudence, says, "Ha! ha! P'lice! Where you find p'lice?"

In the second drawing we see why the noise is more than commonly distressing, for it represents a bedroom in the indignant father's house, where a "sick boy, tended by his mother, is suffering from nervous fever."

I dwell at some length upon these drawings, because they greatly aided Mr. Bass in his efforts to put a stop to some extent—alas! only to some extent—to a serious public nuisance. The Bill which that gentleman carried through Parliament still requires amendment before the author, the musician, the artist, or the tradesman even, can pursue his calling in the peace so essential to success.

An eminent artist friend of mine lived in a part of the town where organ-grinders greatly congregate. The interruptions to his work were constant and terrible. After finding that remonstrance, threats of the police, and other inducements, failed to procure relief, he armed himself with a pea-shooter, with which he practised upon his lay figure until he acquired considerable skill in the use of it; and when he considered he was enough of a marksman, he stood by his shutter window and waited; not for long, for the notes of "Champagne Charley is my name"—a favourite melody some years ago—pierced his ears from "an instrument of torture" opposite to his window. Through a narrow aperture made by the shutter the pea-shooter was projected, a smart blow on the cheek of the organ-grinder stopped "Champagne Charley" in the middle of one of his notes; the man rubbed his face and looked about him, up and down and round about, with an expression of pained surprise pleasant to behold. He then took up the tune where he had left it, and had produced a few more notes when a blow upon the grinding hand, and another almost instantly on his face, again stopped the performance. "It was very gratifying," said my friend, "to study the puzzled expression of the fellow as he looked about for the cause of his trouble." After another attempt to play out his tune, and another salute from the pea-shooter, he shouldered his organ and took himself off. "Yes," said the sportsman, "after a while they found me out, but they couldn't get at me, and now I am never troubled by any of them."

I am writing these pages at Lowestoft, where Leech passed several summer holidays. Under the name of "Sandbath," this place had the honour of appearing in *Punch* as the scene of several humorous incidents, notably of one in which the street-horrors are stigmatized under the heading of "How to Make a Watering-place Pleasant, particularly to Invalids." Time 6.30 a.m. (a hint to the powers that be at Sandbath). The principal performer is an admirably drawn figure of a big burly ruffian—ugliness personified—from whose monstrous mouth one can almost hear "Yah-ha-bloaters!" Two little boys, carrying baskets of shrimps, are yelling "Ser-imps, fine ser-imps!" while two more youths add to the din by ringing bells by way of announcing other delicacies likely to be in request early in the morning. The date of this drawing can be fixed pretty accurately, for I hear from Mr. Adams that several of the sketches in oil exhibited in 1862 were finished at this place, Mr. Adams constantly watching his friend as he worked.

To the unexaggerated truth of the incident I can speak, for the cry of "Bloaters!" arouses me every morning, and precisely at the time indicated by Leech. Added to this, even as I write about the organ-grinder detested of Leech, comes one, as if in revenge, under my window; and in reply to my threat of police, I am told to "go and *find* a policeman"—an impossibility, as the wretch well knows, for there is but one in Sandbath—as far as my observation goes—and he never appears in this part of it.

A petition, very numerously signed by eminent members of all the professions, and by others, was a formidable weapon in Mr. Bass's hands in his crusade against street musicians and other peace-breakers. The Bill passed both Houses, and became law. Leech signalized the success by an admirable drawing called "The Rival Barrels."

"Three cheers for Bass and his barrel of beer, and out with the foreign ruffian and his barrel-organ."

One of Mr. Bass's draymen is using a cask of beer in the form of a weapon as he rolls it against a foreign organ-grinder, who finds himself perilously near the edge of a cliff at Dover or Folkestone, *en route* from the country he has tormented so long. The brutal Italian scowls and threatens as the barrel rolls upon him, but we feel he must go; the stalwart, good-humoured drayman is too much for him.

If—as I feel sure—the brilliant powers possessed by Leech were certain to be attended by a highly sensitive and nervous organization, absolute tranquillity and ease of mind were required for the exercise of them; but in this unhappy case what do we find? No repose—no cessation—no peace. The conditions under which these wonderful drawings were produced were no doubt to some extent uncontrollable—the public appetite grew with what it fed on; it was not *Punch* only who insisted upon his weekly portion, but numberless publications, stories, biographies, poems, taxed the genius of the popular illustrator.

It was not till I undertook this task that I had any idea of the *quantity* of work done by Leech: to say nothing of the excellence of it, the quantity is astonishing. But surely, I hear my reader say, though *Punch* required ever-recurring contributions, other demands upon the artist were within his own control. There are men, and plenty of them, who would have turned deaf ears to appeals from relatives and friends; but John Leech was not one of those, and I fear it cannot be denied it was to meet pressing solicitation for money from various quarters that we must look to account for the worn brain and the shattered nerves that throbbed with agony at noises which would scarcely have disturbed a healthy man.

For some years before his death he suffered from sleeplessness, and at length he yielded to the suggestion of his friends and the order of his doctor—that change of air and scene should be tried as a remedy. Mark Lemon became his companion, and the two went to Biarritz, staying a short time in Paris on their way.

"That Leech's pencil was not idle on this holiday," says Shirley Brooks, "two well-known pictures will testify. One of them is a general view of that now famous watering-place, with specimens of its curious frequenters. The other is a very remarkable drawing. It represents a bull-fight as seen by a decent Christian gentleman, and, for the first time since the brutal fray was invented, the cold-blooded barbarity and stupidity of the show is depicted without any of the flash and flattery with which it has pleased artists to treat the atrocious scene. That grim indictment of a nation professing to be civilized will be on record for many a day after the offence shall have ceased.

"This brief visit," continues Mr. Brooks, "to the Continent was his last but one. His strength did not increase, and he no longer found pleasure in hunting, of which he had been exceedingly fond, and later he discontinued riding on horseback. He was then not merely advised, but ordered to travel. About this time the great man who had been to him as a brother, the schoolmate of his boyhood, the chief friend of his manhood—Thackeray—died. He told Millais of his presentiment that he, too, should die suddenly, and soon. In the summer of 1864 he went to Homburg, accompanied by his friend, Alfred Elmore, and afterwards he sojourned at Schwalbach. His mind was amused if his body was not strengthened by these visits to new scenery, and his sketch-book was soon filled with memorials, some of which he embodied in his last large *Punch* engraving—a view of the place where the residents of Schwalbach meet to drink the waters, and with figures of illustrious political people.

"Soon after his return he resolved to try what pure fresh English air would do for him, and accompanied by his family he went to Whitby. Several friends were also staying there at the same time, and he wrote to London that he liked the place. In September, on his writing to me that he would prolong his stay if

I and wife would come down, we went, and remained at Whitby till he left it, on the 3rd of October.

"The scenery round Whitby is varied, and some of it is exceedingly fine; and Leech, when we could induce him to leave the painting in oil—to which he devoted far too many hours—enjoyed the drives into the wild moors, and up and down the terrible but picturesque roads; and he was still more delighted with the rich woods, deep glades, and glorious views around Mulgrave Castle. I hoped that good was being done; but it was very difficult to stir him from his pictures, of which he declared he must finish a great number before Christmas. It was not for want of earnest and affectionate remonstrance close by his side, nor for lack of such remonstrance being seconded by myself and others, that he persevered in over-labour at these paintings, which he had undertaken with his usual generosity, in order to provide a very large sum of money *for the benefit of his relatives, not of his own household*. It need hardly be said that he was never pressed for work by his old friend the editor of *Punch*. His contributions to that periodical had not exceeded one half-page engraving for some time, until he volunteered to compose the large Schwalbach picture. Let me note another instance of his kindness to utter strangers. A deputation from the Whitby Institute waited upon him to ask him to attend a meeting, and to speak in promotion of the interests of the association. He was on that day too ill to bear an interview with more than one of the gentlemen, and was, of course, compelled to refuse their request. But it occurred to him that they might think his refusal ungracious (as I am sure they could not), and he sent for all his 'Sketches of Life and Character' from London, and presented them to the Institution."

Amongst the party at Whitby was Mr. George Du Maurier, whose charming drawings are familiar, not only to the readers of *Punch*, but also as excellent illustrations in other newspapers and periodicals; especially good are they in Thackeray's great novel of "Esmond." Du Maurier only made Leech's acquaintance a few months before his death, but he tells me that in the Whitby walks and talks he found him to be the most delightful companion, and the most "lovable" of men. My friend also tells me that he was the last of the craft that shook the hand to which we all owe so much. Du Maurier called upon Leech the day before his death to present a little drawing to him; he seemed "much as usual," and the artists parted, little dreaming that they had parted for ever.

On the day after Mr. Hill's party the weekly dinner of the *Punch* staff took place. Leech attended as usual, but the readiness with which he was wont to make suggestions, or to discuss those already made, seemed to have deserted him. He was dull, silent, and appeared, says Shirley Brooks, "scarcely to understand what was going on"—requiring a question to be repeated two or three times before he could frame a reply to it, and then his answer was often wide of the mark. This condition, I suppose, showed the alternations of the disease that was killing him, for he was perfectly free from such a distressing symptom only the night before the *Punch* dinner, and as free from it, according to Du Maurier, the day before his death.

The journeys abroad, and the Whitby sojourn, even if the sufferer could have been prevailed upon to cease work altogether, came too late. The sword had worn out the scabbard. Leech's conversation and letters after his return from Whitby expressed ardent hope, but feeble conviction, that he had materially benefited by the change of air and scene. I think he knew that his prophecy, so mournfully spoken to Millais by the death-bed of Thackeray, was near its fulfilment. In common with all Leech's friends, I knew that he had suffered from attacks of angina pectoris, or breast pang; but in our ignorance of the serious character of the disease, most of us thought lightly of its attacks. One idea amongst us was that he had strained, and perhaps injured, some muscle in one of his hunting tumbles. That the agony of the spasms was very dreadful we knew, because on one occasion, after a severe attack, he said, "If it had lasted a little longer, I must have died." But how often have sufferers used the same words when they were in no danger whatever!

I approach the end of my endeavour to show my illustrious friend in his true colours, with sad feelings, grievously increased by the conviction that under happier circumstances he might have been the delight of all who did—and did not—know him for many years beyond the time so cruelly shortened. The letter to a friend which follows—written at Kensington after his return from Whitby—gives us in his own melancholy words a sad account of his condition.

"6, The Terrace, Kensington,
"October 6, 1864.

"MY DEAR ——,

"I received your most kind note last night on my return from Whitby in Yorkshire, where I have been with my family since I came from Germany; and I assure you I have so many things to put in order, that to go away from my work would be impossible just now. I was amused with Homburg, and to some extent I think the waters did me some good; but I am sorry to say I can give but a sorry account of my health. Nothing seems to quiet my nervous system, and I suffer still from sleeplessness dreadfully. Alas for Sheldrake! Why, I could not ride him if I had him; anything out of a walk would bring on a spasm that would occasion me to drop from his back. I trust I may be able to ride some time yet, but do not see my way. As for shooting, you would see me disappear amongst the turnips in about five minutes from exhaustion. But, however, I look forward with hope, and with a will, shall try and make myself a better man; and I am not yet incapable, thank God, to enjoy the society of a friend, and hope you will find me out—no, not out, but at home—should you come to London this autumn or winter. You must see a pantomime, you know. I have one great consolation—that the air of Yorkshire did my wife and children great good; and hoping that you and all your kind relations at … are well,

"Believe me,
"Yours faithfully,
"JOHN LEECH."

CHAPTER XXIV.

MILLAIS AND LEECH.

The way to a certain place is said to be paved with good intentions. If that be so, a large space in the pavement must be filled by intentions to write the life of Leech. In the Dean of Rochester—the intimate friend of the artist when known as the Rev. Reynolds Hole—the intention still exists, as I gather from a letter received from him in reply to my appeal for assistance. The Dean tells me he possesses "above a hundred letters" by Leech—one and all denied to me—barred by the "intention," which seems to have come to life again, after being resigned by him many years ago in favour of Dr. John Brown; who in his turn relegated his intention to its place in the pavement.

I think it was about the year 1882 that, when calling on my old friend Sir John Millais, I was introduced to a Mr. Evans, who was presented to me as a literary man engaged in writing the life of Leech—a stranger to Millais in quest of information. Though I felt that Millais, in the genial and hearty way peculiar to him, over-estimated the importance of my assistance in his advice to Mr. Evans to tax my memory, "and he would find the tax paid in full," I promised to try to remember something of interest, and communicate with him further. The result of the "taxation" was a paper, which I sent to the address given to me at Manchester.

Years passed, and as I heard nothing I concluded that the Evans life was abandoned, and thought no more of the matter. Alas! events proved that the Evans intention was destined to take its place amongst the others, for the promoter died; but not till he had collected a quantity of material, to which I have been greatly indebted in writing this memoir. After my interview with Mr. Evans at Millais', I never saw or heard from him, except in acknowledgment of my contribution; and it is strange to me, that with every requisite for the carrying out of the intention, into which, judging from his manner, he entered enthusiastically and lovingly, he should have made such little way with it—probably from ill-health—when the material fell into the hands of Messrs. Bentley, and from theirs into mine.

Amongst the papers I found the following from Sir John Millais, of all the friends of Leech one of the dearest, the most loving and steadfast, and the best able to appreciate his qualities as an artist and a man. In a letter to Mr. Evans —February, 1882—Millais says:

"I knew John Leech intimately, and I think saw more of him than any other of his friends. He was one of the very best gentlemen I ever knew, with an astounding appreciation of everything sad or humorous. He was both manly and gentle, nervous and brave, and the most delightful companion that ever lived. I loved John Leech (and another who is also gone) better than any other friends I have known."

In a further communication, Sir John says:

"I will endeavour to find some letters which may be of interest. Unfortunately, I have given most of them away at the time I received them, many containing sketches; I cannot remember now where they are. I am sure I had more than anyone, as I was for years his daily companion. There is another friend of his—Percival Leigh, attached to *Punch*—whom you do not mention. You should see him, as he could give you a great deal of information. Mr. Adams was a hunting friend, and many times Leech and myself stayed with him. Mr. Parry was the master of the Puckeridge hounds, and most of the hunting sketches were the upshot of scenes in Hertfordshire.

"Leech stayed with me twice in Scotland, and out of those visits came Mr. Briggs's exploits in deer-stalking, salmon-fishing, and grouse-shooting.

"The late Duke of Athole asked him to Blair, and took him for a deer-drive. Previously to that there had been a good deal written in the papers against the Duke, in consequence of his Grace having stopped two University men from crossing the forest; and Leech made a drawing in *Punch* by no means complimentary of the Duke, who was represented turning back the tourists, exclaiming, 'I am the regular Do-Dhu.' But you must turn to *Punch*, and you will find the illustration for yourself. I speak from memory as to the exact words; but I well recollect Leech, in his jocose way, asking me whether I thought he would be safe in the Duke's hands after that squib. I afterwards heard his Grace was delighted with it, and carried the woodcut about in his pocket to show to his friends.

"I have seen Leech make his first sketch (of which I have specimens), and trace them on to the block, scores of times. The first was rapid; but on the wood he was very deliberate, knowing how necessary clearness of execution is to the engraver.

"The late Mr. Trelawney—the intimate friend of Byron and Shelley—speaking one day to me of his recollections, said that Shelley and Leech were the two men he had loved best, and that he cared to know me only because I was a great friend of the man he admired so much."

Here I may interpose to remind my readers that the figure of the sailor in Millais' superb picture of the North-West Passage was painted from Trelawney, who is supposed to say, "It should be done, and England must do

153

it." The man's head, painted with all Millais' power, is a most perfect likeness of Shelley's friend.

Millais goes on to tell us that "some of the happiest days we spent together were at the Peacock Inn at Baslow, in Derbyshire, close to Chatsworth, where every kindness was shown to Leech by the Duke and Sir Joseph Paxton—shooting, fishing, and cricketing."

I again interpose to say that the portrait given as frontispiece to this volume was drawn on one of the "happy days" at the Peacock Inn at Baslow.

"We played together in a match with a neighbouring village, and at a supper which he gave to the teams he sang 'King Death' with becoming gravity, and was much entertained by the local amorous ditties sung by the young farmers."

In further advice to Mr. Evans, Sir John says:

"You cannot dwell too much on his tender anxiety for his wife and children, almost distressing at times to those about him."

The great painter continues:

"I should tell you that he was always careful in his dress, and always went to the best houses for everything he purchased, probably from having early in life discovered the wisdom of such a course—see his satire of everything shoddy—but chiefly from inherent good taste. His choice was so quiet that one only *felt* he was perfectly attired. Leech was six feet high, slim, well but rather delicately made. Strangers felt when they were introduced to him that they were in the presence of a gentleman grave and courteous always, and a merry fellow when harmless fun was demanded. Like Landseer, he had the power of telling a story in the fewest words, and with astonishing effect upon his hearers; but as a rule he was averse to taking the initiative in conversation. He would sit placidly smoking his cigar in an easy-chair, and only chime in to cap what was said by some voluble speaker, and then retire again into the full enjoyment of his weed and silence."

In his evidence before a Committee of the House of Commons which was formed to inquire into the constitution and working of the Royal Academy, with a view to certain changes in that body, Millais said that he thought Leech was deserving of full membership in the institution, for, indeed, said he:

"Very few of us painters will leave behind us such good and valuable work as he has left—work which is in great part historical. His appreciation of the pathetic was as strong as his sense of the ridiculous, and you will never find a bit of false sentiment in anything he did."

Landseer is reported to have said—after expressing enthusiastic admiration of Leech's genius—that the worst thing he ever did deserved to be framed and placed before students as an example for their emulation and improvement. Sir John Millais concludes his remarks upon his friend—remarks for which I am sure my readers will be as grateful as I am—by a few pathetic words heralding the sad and final scene:

"He became so nervous latterly that he used to take my arm when we were walking together, jerking it perceptibly at any sudden noise, or at any vehicle passing rapidly near us; lingering an unnecessary time at the street crossings; and the morning he came from Thackeray's house, on coming downstairs after seeing his dead friend, he said, 'I also shall die suddenly.'

"I arrived from a Continental tour," concludes Millais, "the day of his death, and by arrangement went immediately to his house to dine with him. His wife told me he had been asking for me; but I did not think it wise to disturb him then. A little later I returned, ran upstairs to his bedside, and found him dead."

CHAPTER XXV.

MR. H. O. NETHERCOTE AND JOHN LEECH.

For the following interesting paper my readers are indebted to Mr. Nethercote, of Moulton Grange, Northamptonshire, who sent it to my predecessor, Mr. Evans, amongst whose Leech material I found it. As Mr. Nethercote's anecdotes were intended for publication, I reproduce them without alteration or abbreviation. Mr. Nethercote and Leech were at Charterhouse together.

"Leech," says his friend, "was the most popular boy in the school, and the margins of his grammars were a delight to boyish eyes. After leaving Charterhouse I lost sight of him for many years; but through the medium of our common friend Reynolds, now Canon Hole, we came together again when he was living in Brunswick Square, and we frequently met at each other's houses. On one occasion, after telling me of his sufferings from street bands, he said:

"'May I come to you with wife and family for a few days? I am dying of "Dixie's Land."'

"He came, and the very first day after dinner, on taking our evening stroll round the garden, our ears were greeted with the hateful tune! The village band had just mastered the homicidal air, and were inadvertently making themselves *particeps crimines* in the murder of my friend. I shall never forget his delightful smile as, when the doleful tune burst upon our ears, he said:

"'Ah, well! "Dixie's Land" in Brunswick Square and "Dixie's Land" at Moulton Grange are two very different tunes; in the latter case a mile of atmosphere intervenes between it and me, and in the former I was in the very bowels of it.'

"He was fond of going to see a meet with hounds, but he was no rider. He once asked me to sell him a horse I was riding, on the ground of its apparent quietness. I declined doing this because it was not right in its wind.

"'All the better,' said he; 'it will not be able to run away far;' and he bought it.

"He was fond of being here (at Moulton Grange), and used to enjoy taking quiet rides along the lanes, and over the many-acred, well-gated grass fields, full of heavy Hertford and Devon cattle; and many a delightful chat have I had with him *in rebus Punchibus*, its contributors, artists, publishers, editors, etc. I am inclined to think that the man he liked best in the world was R. Hole, and then Thackeray and Millais; but of course I cannot say this with any certainty."

I stop Mr. Nethercote's narrative for a moment for Mrs. Leech to be heard; that lady assured Canon Hole—now Dean of Rochester—after Leech's death, that the two men whom her husband loved best in the world were himself and Millais. Thackeray was asked to name the man he loved above all others, and he named Leech; but on another occasion, when he was asked the same question by his daughter, as recorded in Fitzgerald's "Memoirs," he said:

"Why, Fitz, to be sure; and next to him Brookfield."

We will now listen again to Mr. Nethercote, who says:

"By his desire I accompanied him one night to see 'Lord Dundreary,' and I shall never forget his dismay on seeing that neither the farce nor the acting had 'fetched' me. He could not understand my feeling that the whole thing was non-natural, and that no lord who ever lived was half so great a fool as Lord Dundreary.

"On one occasion he was staying at Moulton Grange on the eve of the great fight between Tom Sayers and Heenan. A lady of great beauty, one of the party, was enlarging overnight on the brutality of all prize-fights, and expressed a hope that this fight might be prevented. On hearing of Sayers' conduct in the fight, the lady could not help expressing her admiration of his bravery, whereon Leech made a charming sketch of his fair friend crowning Sayers with a laurel-wreath, and entitled it 'Beauty crowning Valour.'

"I need not say how greatly the sketch is valued by its possessors.

"Leech used to like hearing his work criticised by friendly amateurs, and seemed to take in and, as it were, masticate their comments.

"I remember once, over our after-dinner cigar, telling him that I considered he failed in portraying the periphery of a wheel—that he made it over-fluffy—and failed also in drawing a stake and bound fence.

"The latter he admitted, and begged me to find him a model to study. This I did, and an excellent 'stake and bound' appeared in the *Punch* of the following Wednesday.

"He stuck to his wheel, and doubtless he was right and I was wrong.

"The last letter I received from him was in reply to an invitation to come for a week's shooting. I knew that he had been ill, and hoped it might do him good. His answer was:

"'Shoot, my dear Nethercote; I couldn't walk round a turnip.'

"When that was written the end was not far off. The news reached me as I left home to hunt, and heavy indeed was my heart all that day, and for many a succeeding one, and still is when I think of him, the warmest-hearted, most generous, gracious, kindly, hospitable, endearing friend that man ever had.

"Such are some of the recollections of my dear friend, written off in a hurry. If they prove of any use to you, you are most welcome to them.

"H. O. Nethercote.

"October 12, 1885."

Mr. Ashby Sterry.

The name which heads the few words below is one that is very familiar as the writer of many charming verses; and it is no wonder that Mr. Evans, on discovering the sonnet addressed to Miss Rosie Leech, should have mistaken the source of its inspiration, the more readily, as Miss Leech was christened Ada Rose.

In the belief that my readers will be glad to have the verses, and Mr. Ashby Sterry's account of their production, I add them to Mr. Sterry's sympathetic appreciation of Leech.

"For as long as I can remember, I have had the most profound admiration for the genius of John Leech," says Mr. Sterry; "and he gave me as much delight in my childhood as he subsequently did when I became a man. I am grieved to say that I hardly knew him at all; it was many years after his death that I became connected with *Punch*. I should be most happy for you to quote the lines to Miss Rosie Leech; they, however, do not refer to John Leech's daughter. Several girls that I knew some years ago reminded me forcibly of the works of various artists. I sketched their portraits in sonnets, and added their Christian name to the surname of the master they represented."

Rosie was emphatically a "Leech girl" in all respects, and one that he would have gloried in drawing.

"MISS ROSIE LEECH.

"Down on the sands there strolls a merry maid,
    Aglow with ruddy health and gladsome glee;
    She breasts the breezes of the summer sea,
And lets each zephyr trifle with each braid;
Laughs gaily as her petticoats evade
    Her girlish grasp and wildly flutter free,
    As, bending to some boisterous decree,
The neatest foot and ankle are displayed.
Her rounded youthful figure you may trace
    Half pouting, as rude Boreas unfurls
A wealth of snowy frillery and lace,
    A glory of soft golden-rippled curls.
Comes blushing with a rare unconscious grace,
    The bonniest of England's bonny girls!"

MR. H. CHOLMONDELEY PENNELL AND LEECH.

"PUCK ON PEGASUS."

Mr. C. Pennell (*loquitur*): "My acquaintance began with his making some illustrations for my book 'Puck on Pegasus.' I found him liberal to generosity in all his professional dealings with me. Indeed, I have since ascertained that, seeing I was a débutant in literature, he only let me pay him about half his usual price—a generosity in which he was equalled by my friend Mr. John Tenniel. The charming drawings of these two inimitable artists on wood were, I have not the slightest doubt, the principal cause of the success of the verses to which they were so unequally mated.

"The Athenæum, I recollect, whilst using the scalping-knife freely on the letterpress, observed that 'the illustrations were of Leech's loveliest.' Naturally, I have always felt towards Leech and Tenniel the gratitude which a young author owes to men who, already famous themselves, so frankly and generously first lent him a helping hand.

"I think Mr. Tenniel and Mr. Leech were at the time I speak of great friends, and I remember their once asking me to go down somewhere to hunt with them—an invitation which I have since regretted not being able to accept. Leech was an enthusiast about hunting, and hence his admirable and accurate delineations of horses and hunting scenes.

"He was a decidedly handsome man; tall, square, and well built, and in manners delightfully genial and frank. I was young when I knew him, and had not had much experience of the world; but I have often thought since that he was one of the most fascinating men it has ever been my good fortune to meet.

"Out of the artists whose pencils graced the pages of 'Puck on Pegasus,' not only those I have mentioned, but also Sir John Millais and Sir Noël Paton, are, as everyone knows, striking instances of exceptional—well, what shall I call it, to spare their blushes?—say 'good looks.' Since I last met the 'Queen's Limner for Scotland,' his hair has become gray, but, notwithstanding, as I told Lady Paton a few weeks ago, her husband is still the handsomest man in North Britain.

"The only little special circumstance I can recall of Leech's 'individualism,' so to speak, is the fondness he had for sitting half on the table—one leg resting on the ground, and one dangling—the attitude in which he is represented in the photograph I have of him."

As the foregoing—found amongst Mr. Evans' Leech material—was evidently intended for publication, I make no scruple in presenting it to my readers. Without presuming to pose as a literary critic, I venture to differ from the author of "Puck on Pegasus" where he relegates his rhymes so far to the limbo of poetical failures as to claim for their chief merit that of having been the cause of some most admirable illustrations. Mr. Cholmondeley Pennell was unusually fortunate in all his illustrators; but surely such brilliantly clever youthful efforts as "Puck on Pegasus" displayed well deserved their good fortune. I confess I was disappointed in finding two drawings only which, from internal evidence, I can attribute to Leech; these, and, indeed, most of the others, strange to say, are unsigned.

Readers of Longfellow will, I think, agree with me that the "Song of In-the-Water" is an admirable imitation of the manner of the American poet's "Hiawatha," without the caricature, not to say vulgarity, which so often disfigures those attempts.

The "Song of In-the-Water" is short, and I am tempted to treat my readers to the whole of it.

I also note the delightful little initial letter W, pictorially rendered, evidently by Doyle:

"When the summer night descended
 Sleepy, on the white witch water,
 Came a lithe and lovely maiden,
 Gazing on the silent water—
    Gazing on the gleaming river—
 With her azure eyes and tender
 On the river glancing forward,

Till the laughing wave sprang upward,
   Upward from his reedy hollow
     With the lily in his bosom,
   With his crown of water lilies—
     Curling every dimpled ripple
As he sprang into the starlight,
As he clasped her charmed reflection
     Glowing to his crystal bosom,
As he whispered, 'Fairest, fairest,
     Rest upon this crystal bosom!'
And she straightway did accordin';—
Down into the water stept she,
     Down into the wavering river,
Like a red deer in the sunset—
Like a ripe leaf in the autumn:
From her lips, as rose-buds snow-filled,
     Came a soft and dreamy murmur,
     Softer than the breath of summer,
       Softer than the murm'ring river,
       Than the cooing of Cushawa—
Sighs that melted as the snows melt,
     Silently and sweetly melted;
Sounds that mingled with the crisping
     Foam upon the billow resting:
Yet she spoke not, only murmured.

"From the forest shade primeval,
  Piggey-Wiggey looked out at her;
     He, the very Youthful Porker—
     He, the Everlasting Grunter—
Gazed upon her there, and wondered!
     With his nose out, Rokey Pokey—
     And his tail up, Curley Wurley—
Wondered what on earth the joke was,
Wondered what the girl was up to—
What the deuce her little game was,
Why she didn't squeak and grunt more!
     And she floated down the river
     Like a water-proof Ophelia;
FOR HER CRINOLINE SUSTAINED HER."

We may look, and look in vain, through the long list of Leech's delightful
creations for anything more lovely, more exquisitely dainty, than this floating

damsel, with grace and charm in every line of her. I am sure my readers will join me in gratitude to Mr. Pennell for having given occasion for a picture that is "a joy for ever."

Leech's remaining drawing illustrates a poem entitled "Rejected Addresses," not in any way, I think, intended as a parody of any of the celebrated "Rejected Addresses" of Messrs. Smith—addresses, it will be remembered, that were written in the manner of various poets who flourished early in this century. Mr. Pennell deals with a certain Alderman, a Sir Toby, who was

"An Alderman of the very first degree,
  But neither wife nor son had he:
     He had a daughter fair—
And often said her father, 'Cis,
You shall be dubbed "my Lady," Miss,
     When I am dubbed Lord Mayor.'"

"Sir Gobble Grist" was the aged swain of parental choice, but, as is not uncommon in such cases, the choice was not favoured by one of the parties concerned in it. The Alderman was, however, peremptory, for he says to the pretty Cis:

"'The day I don the gown and chain,
  In Hymen's modern Fetter Lane
     You wed Sir Gobble Grist;
And whilst with pomp and pageant high
I scrape, and strut, and star it by
St. George's in the East, you'll try
     St. George's in the West.'

"Oh, vision of parental pride!
  Oh, blessed Groom to such a Bride!
     Oh, happy Lady Cis!
Yet sparks must always strike the match,
And miss may chance to lose her 'catch,'
     Or he may catch *a miss*!

"Such things do happen, here and there
  When knights are old, and nymphs are fair,
     And who can say they don't?
When Worldly takes the gilded pill,
And Dives stands and says, 'I will,'
     AND BEAUTY SAYS, 'I WON'T.'

*   *   *   *   *

"Alas! that beaus will lose their spring,
And wayward belles refuse to 'ring,'
        Unstruck by Cupid's dart!
Alas that—must the truth be told—
Yet oft'ner has the archer sold
The 'white and red' to touch 'the gold,'
        And Diamonds trumped the Heart!

"That luckless heart! too soon misplaced,
Why is it that parental taste,
On sagest calculation based,
        So rarely pleases Miss?
Let those who can the riddle read;
For me, I've no idea indeed,
        No more, perhaps, had Cis.

"It may be that she found Sir G.
Less tender than a swain should be,— Young—sprightly—
        witty—gay.
It might have been she thought his hat
Or head too round, or square, or flat,
        Or empty—who can say?

    *   *   *   *   *

"I know not! but the Parson waited,
  The Bridegroom swore, the Groomsmen rated,
        Till two o'clock or near;—
Then home again in rage and wrath,
Whilst pretty Cis—was rattling North
        With Jones the Volunteer!"

Surely the poet has no occasion to blush for these verses, or to think that they
needed Leech's aid to preserve them. To me they seem admirable of their
kind, and well worthy of affording employment for Leech's inimitable pencil;
and how perfectly has he realized for us the happy pair! Let us hope that
pretty Cis has made a prudent choice in the handsome Volunteer, whose
uneasy glance conveys a fear that the journey 'due North' may still be
interrupted. To those who desire to read sprightly verse, and to see the verse
illustrated with very uncommon perfection by such artists as Doyle, Millais,
Tenniel, Sir Noël Paton, and others, I heartily commend "Puck on Pegasus."

On Tuesday, the 25th of October, 1864, I dined at the house of Mr. Hills, in
Queen Ann Street. The party consisted of several gentlemen, most of whose
names I forget. I think Landseer and Millais were amongst the guests. I am

sure Leech was, for I sat next to him. I cannot say I noticed much difference in his appearance; he was perhaps even quieter than usual, and when he joined in general conversation I fancied I noticed a slight change in his deep voice, which seemed to me to have a kind of far-away sound in it, more noticeable still when he spoke to me. I heard he had not been well, and, in reply to my inquiry, he said he should be well enough if he could get away from the horrible noises that never seemed to cease in his neighbourhood. Back and front of his house, he said, noises of all kinds were incessant; his servant's time was taken up in sending away street musicians; the cries of the hawkers were awful, work was impossible to him except under agonizing conditions—a butcher's cart passed and repassed his house repeatedly with a dog in it that barked continually. He then mentioned other nuisances, and concluded his grievances with a sentence which I can never forget. "Rather, Frith," he said, "than continue to be tormented in this way, I would prefer to go to the grave where there is no noise." Before that day week his desire was accomplished, his ever-to-be-honoured grave had received him, and he was deaf to all noises for evermore.

Leech's doctors had warned him against excitement of any kind; he was forbidden to ride on horseback or to walk rapidly; and he was told that, if he would cease to work, and dismiss all anxiety from his mind, they had good hope of his recovery. Cease to work and dismiss anxiety! What vain words to a man who was consumed by the desire to raise money, which nothing but work would bring! And for whom were these dying energies put forth? Clearly not for himself or "his own household."

The day before his death Leech went to see Dr. Quain, who again prescribed absolute rest as his only chance. And how did the poor fellow follow this advice? He went home and wrote to the *Punch* office, saying that a messenger might be sent for a drawing in progress, which "he would finish if he could." Strange to say, the fancy was as bright and the imagination as powerful as ever, and, for the moment, the hand itself had lost none of its cunning; but the physical strength failed utterly, and the pencil fell from that wonderful hand for ever. The messenger came, and was sent empty away.

On the day of his death—having spent the rest of the previous day, after his failure to complete the *Punch* drawing, in bed—he begged to be allowed to draw. "It would amuse me," he said. A medical friend who was present gave a reluctant permission, and seeing no immediate appearance of danger, the doctor left him to his amusement. "Instead, however, of beginning at once," says Miss Leech, "he threw himself upon a couch in the room, and after a little while he was persuaded to go to bed and keep himself perfectly quiet. This he did, but scarcely had he composed himself for sleep than he suddenly started up and, calling to his father and sister, fell back and expired in their arms without a sigh."

Thus, on the 29th of October, 1864, died John Leech, done to death by overwork in his anxiety for others, who, let us hope, were worthy of the sacrifice. It is not too much to say that the death of this inimitable artist was a sorrow to all English-speaking people, and no less to many foreign peoples, who—"as one touch of nature makes the whole world kin"—fully relished the beauty, truth, and humour of all Leech's work. Of this we have ample proof in the elaborately appreciative remarks of French and German writers. Among the former, M. Ernest Chesnau, in the *Gazette des Beaux Arts* of June, 1875, has an exhaustive article on Leech and his works—too long for reproduction here. Of the loving sympathy felt by his German brethren, the following tribute from the German *Punch*—the *Kladderadatsch*—offers ample evidence. It is entitled "A Cypress Branch for the Tomb of John Leech."

"Poor John! Thy German brethren, too, stand in the shape of a weeping willow at thy grave, for our locks are turned to mourning branches that droop down over thy simple cross. Ungrudgingly we behold thy glory, thy 'like nature' which stirred up the foul carp-pond of life. We remember thy fox-hunting and angling gentlemen, thy ladies, the pretty ones and the declining, thy blue stockings, thy gentlemen, thy volunteers, thy sportsmen, thy Flunkeiana, and thy immortal Mr. Briggs, this pearl of English *bonhommie*. Mr. Punch, too, whose greatest ornament thou wert, sits mourning on thy tomb. He has cast off his merry Punchinello costume, and is nothing but a sorrowing old man. Farewell, merry John, thou boy of endless good-humour.

"We erect this little monument in thy own spirit, with an eye that laughs through tears, for after thou hadst conquered the first bitter pangs of death, thou must surely at thy last moment have smiled at leaving this miserable world."

A Cypress Branch for the Tomb of John Leech.

The English journals vied with each other in expressions of sorrow for this irreparable loss. The death of Garrick, said Dr. Johnson, "eclipsed the gaiety of nations." How much more truly this may be said of the premature death of Leech! Never was man so loved and honoured by his personal friends, never was a man's death more sincerely mourned than that of "dear, kind John Leech" by those who had the delightful privilege of knowing intimately all the endearing qualities of his heart and mind. See what that great man, who was so soon to follow him to the grave, says, and think what the simple words imply! Says Dickens, in a letter to Forster written a few days after Leech's death, "I have not done my number ('Our Mutual Friend'). This death of poor Leech has put me out woefully."

It was predicted that Leech's death would be death to *Punch*. How false and foolish that prophecy was, none knew so well as Leech himself; but while admitting to the full the great talent of the present *Punch* staff of artists, it cannot be denied that Leech's place is vacant, and I assume the prophetic mantle and proclaim (I hope mistakenly) that it will never be filled. It should always be borne in mind that though it is impossible to exaggerate the benefit that *Punch* derived from Leech's pencil, the artist is also deeply indebted to *Punch* for the exceptional opportunities the peculiar character of the paper offered for the display of his powers. The fact is, the paper and the illustrations were exactly suited to each other, and always worked harmoniously together.

That Leech's death would be keenly felt by all connected with *Punch* goes without saying, and if tears are evidences of grief, those that fell from the eyes of the whole of the staff as they stood round Leech's grave gave full assurance of their sorrow.

On the 3rd of November, by a notice in the daily papers, the public were informed that the funeral of John Leech would take place at Kensal Green on the following day. At two o'clock on the afternoon of the 4th, great crowds of people lined the ways from the chapel to the grave, which was already surrounded by the friends and acquaintances of the dead. The pall-bearers were Mark Lemon, Shirley Brooks, Tom Taylor, J. E. Millais, R.A., Horace Mayhew, M. Evans (Bradbury and Evans, of *Punch*), John Tenniel, F. C. Burnand, Samuel Lucas, and Henry Silver (all members of the staff or contributors to *Punch*). These were followed by John Leech, the artist's father; Dr. Quain, poor Leech's unwearied attendant in his illness; Charles Keene, George Du Maurier, and others, all more or less associated with Leech in their relation to *Punch*. In attendance were Charles Dickens, W. H. Russell, Perceval Leigh, Edmund Yates, Charles F. Adams, German Reed, H. K. Browne ('Phiz'), Thomas Landseer, A.R.A., George Cruikshank, Godfrey Turner, Creswick (the tragedian), Marcus Stone, J. Phillip, R.A., W. P. Frith, R.A., and many others. The red coats of two soldiers made bright spots amongst the sombre crowd. The service for the dead was read by the Rev. S. R. Hole, now Dean of Rochester, whose warm friendship for Leech distressingly affected him in his delivery of the solemn passages in the burial service. The last words had scarcely ceased when we crowded together, and without a dry eye amongst us, as we took our farewell look into the resting-place of the man we loved so well. One tomb only divides the graves of Thackeray and Leech. Of both these men it may be justly said that, like Saul and Jonathan of old, "they were beautiful in their lives," and but a short time and a small space divide them in their deaths.

Leech's wife and children soon followed him to the grave; and though, to the surprise and regret of all who knew of the immense mass of work that he produced, he was unable to leave even a moderate fortune behind him, it is satisfactory to know that his family did not suffer. Anything approaching privation was warded off by means which it is not necessary to particularize.

The whole world is the inheritor under the will of Leech; and what a legacy he has bequeathed! Posterity will be able to study us in our habits as we lived, in our pleasures and our pains, in our follies and eccentricities, in our sports and amusements—in short, in every condition of life, high and low. A type, or types, of every class, from the very poor to the very rich, from the beggar to the King, spring perfect from Leech's pencil. He revels in beauty; tenderness and manly strength combine in his works, as they did in himself, a love of what is good and pure, and a hatred of the ignoble and the base is shown in all he drew, and in every act of his private life. My endeavour in these pages has been to convey to those to whom Leech will be but a name, as clear an idea as lay in my power of the "life and character" of the author of the matchless works which will be a delight for all time. Death only sanctifies the loving memory in which Leech will be held by those who knew him. The kindly and intelligent of future generations will, I hope and believe, not only appreciate the humour and character, the fun and frolic, in Leech's drawings, but discover also the delightful nature of their producer in many a tender touch, in many a good-natured rendering of matter that was susceptible in other hands of severe or vulgar treatment; and if I can create for him something of the affectionate regard in the future that is universally felt for him in the present, my object in writing this imperfect memoir will be attained.

CPSIA information can be obtained
at www.ICGtesting.com
Printed in the USA
LVHW051326250820
664152LV00012B/1042